# RAW *Deal*

## JACKSON KANE

Raw Deal © 2020 by Jackson Kane



Raw Deal is a work of fiction. All names, characters, events and places found therein are either from the author's imagination or used fictitiously. Any similarity to persons alive or dead, actual events, locations, or organizations is entirely coincidental and not intended by the author.

For information, contact the publisher, Hot Tree Publishing.
www.hottreepublishing.com

EDITING: HOT TREE EDITING
COVER DESIGNER: BOOKSMITH DESIGN
FORMATTING: RMGRAPHX

E-BOOK ISBN: 978-1-925853-82-7
PAPERBACK ISBN: 978-1-925853-83-4

Blow Out (Steel Veins 1)
Burn Up (Steel Veins 2)
Raw Deal (Steel Veins 3)
My Holiday Secret
Billionaire Takes All

# Author's Note:

No other reading is necessary.
This standalone takes place after the events of *Burn Up*.

After a divisive philosophy shift and a dramatic change to the Steel Veins leadership four years ago, the cruelest, worst members broke off to form their own MC—the Broken Veins. Pissed off and ruthless as hell, the Broken Veins want nothing more than to see the world burn.

*If you like spine-tingling sex and blood-boiling violence, you've come to the right place!*

This novel contains graphic situations. Raw, edgy, and violent in parts. With gritty, hot sex as well. There are also sensitive situations depicted as well as potential PTSD triggers. Any readers who feel they should not venture into a story told with a real edge on reality in the violent word of an MC should consider this warning before reading…

# Prologue
## MASON



"Tell us about Elisha, Mason," the federal agent asked me again.

Through the chaos and bloodshed that nipped at our heels every step of the way, Elisha's dark eyes were the first thing that came into focus in my head and in my heart. Despite the fact that it'd been months since I'd seen her, I would never forget that they were the subtlest brown I'd ever seen.

Elisha had a beauty I'd never thought possible before. Up close, with only breath and heat between us, those brown eyes glimmered like stardust.

Then the rest of her flooded me. Her silky brown skin was soft and smooth to the touch. From the tight bun she wore her straightened black hair in to her ginger-kissed lips, every inch and curve of her slim body was etched into my memory.

And of course, her bright blue-and-white inhaler.

Then there was the sex. The sweaty, filthy, raucous sex of two people who spat in the face of reason and defied fate at every turn.

I wouldn't tell them all that. No, that was mine.

"Mason." This time it was a different voice that called my name. A royal pain in my ass named Harris. "Tell us about the girl."

I cracked a smile that wasn't meant for them. It was for Elisha. She wasn't in the room to see it, but wherever she was, I hoped she could feel it.

"Nothing to tell really." I shrugged.

Aside from the fact that I wouldn't be alive right now if not for her. I'd either be dead or wishing I was.

In hushed tones, they conversed between themselves.

"Don't be coy, jackass," Harris shot back. "Gang war, the toppling of an entire MC, gunrunning cartels—you know how serious this all is. You could be in a tremendous amount of trouble, Mason."

"I guess we'll have to see, then, won't we?"

"I only have one more question for him before you bring him back to his cell." Harris closed my file dramatically. "Was she worth losing everything for?"

It took me a moment to reply. I wanted to picture her smiling back at me one more time before I answered.

"Everything?" I laughed. "You mean my freedom and my life?"

They still didn't get it. How could they? Elisha and I were just words on a page to them. Strip all that away and I'd still have the time we spent together. No one could take that away from me. Not the FBI or the Broken Veins.

She saved me in more ways than they could imagine.

Elisha was the lighthouse in the storm of my soul. "To answer your question: I don't regret a damn thing."

# Chapter 1
## ELISHA

FIVE MONTHS AGO

Once I got on the interstate in Kentucky, it was almost impossible to miss the Broken Veins Motorcycle Club. This was the most efficient route to get from Philly to Arkansas, so it was only a matter of patience. I'd been parked along the road, knowing they'd eventually catch up and pass me.

And when they did, I'd catch Mason.

Once I found the connection between Mason and the Broken Veins, I'd done a tremendous amount of research on that MC. They were ruthless, especially that particular chapter. Countless charges of aggravated assault, rape, murder, drug trafficking… the list went on and on.

I'd already started to have doubts about what I was even doing here, when I'd seen the Broken Veins in my mirror several miles out. Kenneth and I had brought in some tough fugitives before, but never anyone like this.

Still, I'd take an angry biker gang over being back in the office with Kenneth and Chelsea. I fumed at the thought of them lying to my face for however long the affair had been going on.

Two near parallel lines of leather-clad bikers weaved through traffic like a rolling thunderstorm of chrome and rubber. They overtook family sedans and other commuters as if they were standing still. The ones who wouldn't or couldn't get out of the way fast enough received a knuckle rap on their hood from each biker who passed them.

Witnessing the Broken Veins' callousness and brutality on the road made the inklings of doubt in the back of my head chirp up a little louder.

Could I really handle this on my own?

These bikers were a crackling storm cloud on a sunny day; every aspect of them emanated danger. I began to ask myself why I was even taking this bounty. Getting away from Kenneth and the office was one thing, but going toe-to-toe with a vicious gang of thugs?

What was I trying to prove?

"Incoming call from… Kenneth" sounded over my car's speakers.

I sighed with exasperation. "Ignore."

Kenneth had blown up my phone so much that it was making my Bluetooth ache. I was on the verge of outright disabling it, but I was waiting to hear back from a few other leads I'd been chasing down.

The image of my now *ex*-fiancé, Kenneth, thrashing around on top of our receptionist, Chelsea, had chased me across three states. It was only last night that I caught them. The wound was too fresh for me to talk to him right now.

No matter how hard I pushed down the gas pedal, I

couldn't outrun it. I knew I couldn't dodge Kenneth forever, but even the *thought* of the sound of his voice made me both sick and angry.

I'd have to deal with him at some point, and it was going to be messy. Now wasn't the time. I had other things to worry about.

Scanning my mirrors, I thought I spotted my fugitive near the back of the pack. The rider, like the others, wore no helmet and a black leather vest adorned with brightly colored patches. Mason's vest was left open, the wind sending it flapping behind him like great leather bat wings.

Despite all my research, the only picture of Mason that turned up was the same dated mugshot that was clipped to his file. It was almost like someone had gone through and wiped him from most of the databases. Mason basically ceased to exist after he skipped bail two years ago.

I was chasing a ghost.

Mason blazed past my rearview, then my side mirror, then disappeared. I freaked out for a second, thinking I'd somehow lost him in my blind spot. He abruptly appeared two lanes closer, riding next to me. He was so close that, if my window were down, we could've touched hands.

I gasped, sinking low in my seat. Did he somehow know I was tracking him down?

Drifting slowly behind me, I saw the car he swerved around that put him right next to me. It eased my worry. I hadn't even started following him yet. Of course he couldn't possibly know who I was.

I couldn't tell if he actually slowed down or if that was

just the rate the Broken Veins were traveling. Whatever the reason, I used the opportunity to steal glances at the man. I needed to confirm that he really was the fugitive I was looking for.

The dusty golden yellow wheat fields that blanketed the far side of the road behind Mason made him look like a mirage. The midday sun caught his bare chest and stomach at just the right angle to set his tawny beige skin on fire. The glistening rough lines of his sculpted muscles carved hard angles of deep shadow across his torso.

*Jesus.* I swallowed, feeling a lump rise in my throat. *That tiny photo left a lot to the imagination.*

His layered walnut hair danced like heavy smoke on the wind. Occasional strands fleetingly caught on the rugged stubble that encased his strong, square jaw. My eyes flickered over the many tattoos that were etched into his summer-worn flesh.

I felt my pulse quicken and the corner of my bottom lip slide between my teeth. My eyes darted away again; it was all I could do just to stay on the road. In my line of work, I thought I'd seen every variety of criminal, but I'd never seen a man like him before.

When I turned back, he was looking right at me. My eyes flared in surprise. He must have seen that, because his mouth cracked into a wicked grin.

Mason wore dangerous confidence as easily as he wore the black-and-white printed bandanna around his neck. From behind his dark shades, I could swear he winked at me. He twisted the throttle, and his engine screamed to life.

The quick acceleration lifted the front wheel of his vintage black Harley Davidson off the ground for a moment. Then he bombed forward and rejoined his pack.

I exhaled watching him go, feeling a little exhausted. Even though I hadn't dealt with bikers before, I knew they couldn't all be like him. I'd never found the biker lifestyle appealing. However, after seeing him up close, I could understand how some women could get caught up in it. Mason was the epitome of unyielding outlaw freedom.

*Focus, Elisha.*

My white SUV wasn't built for speeds like the rockets-on-wheels the Broken Veins were riding. After they blew by, it was a struggle just to keep up and not lose them completely.

I didn't have to tail them for long. I'd caught up with the bikers just before lunch and knew they'd have to stop eventually. When they did, that was my window to grab Mason.

Soon enough, they slowed, pulling off the highway and into a small state-run rest area. I kept my distance, always maintaining an eyeline on Mason. I didn't come this far to have him slip away. Justified or not, it was the truth. He wasn't just a handsome biker; he was also a half-million-dollar bounty.

Kenneth and I had been together for ten years, ever since we graduated from high school. Everything I had was jointly owned with him. Our cars, the house, even the bounty hunter company we'd started a few years ago was in both our names. I thought we were building a life together.

How could I have been so blind? It made me both sad and furious!

I couldn't see any way that this breakup wouldn't be extremely messy, and Kenneth had a lot more legal connections than I did. If he was feeling petty enough, he could try to take everything from me, and I just wouldn't have enough money to hire a lawyer who could match his.

The money I'd stand to make on this bounty was the only chance of equaling the playing field. It was the only way I could fight Kenneth, if it came to that.

It didn't matter how terrifying the Broken Veins were. I didn't have the luxury of quitting.

The off-ramp split into two short roads, one for cars and the other for big trucks. There was a liquor store/welcome center/restaurant sandwiched between the two. The bikers took the former, and I took the latter. That put me at the back of the building with a fantastic vantage point on the restrooms.

Now all I had to do was wait and be ready.

While the bikers got lunch, I reviewed Mason's file and ate the food I'd packed. He'd been arrested a few times, all vehicle theft related. The most recent one was a borderline misdemeanor.

Most of the charges were dropped when he was in his midtwenties, but North Carolina still wanted him real bad. Bad enough to issue a bounty that was worth *half a million dollars*. Something seemed odd about the whole thing, but I triple-checked and made sure.

Mason Stone was a wanted man, and I was going to be

the one to bring him in.

Kenneth rejected this bounty before I'd even had the chance to review the file. He'd been doing that far too frequently lately. We were supposed to be partners. We'd have to reevaluate those roles when I came back to the office. My mind cascaded into anger and worry over Kenneth's *latest* cheating incident.

That's not why I took this job, I reminded myself. I was here to catch a fugitive, not dwell on the past. I forced all that out and resumed poring over the little info there was about Mason.

He didn't have much in the way of family. His mother died when he was young, and there was some mention of a sister, but that was about it. There was only one real lead, and it was written in pencil by one of the Carver, North Carolina, police officers. 'Presumed association with the outlaw motorcycle club the Broken Veins.'

His file almost looked like it had been scrubbed by some other government agency, like the CIA, NSA, or feds. That wasn't a big deal, though. The government redacted information in files all the time.

"Incoming text from… Julie" came through the car speakers. Julie was an old friend of mine. We were cadets together in the police academy. She was the only one who stood up for me when I was 'disqualified' because of misfiled paperwork. Apparently being black *and* female was still too progressive for Lawrence County, Alabama.

Some movement near the bathroom had my eyes snapping back up. Mason walked in and closed the door behind him. The text message sounded through the speakers. "Broken Veins are headed to an annual club-wide meet up just outside of Little Rock, Arkansas."

*Damn.* I'd known the where, just not the why. If Mason made it to the meet, there would be too many bikers around for me to even get near him. I grabbed my gun and cuffs and hurriedly climbed out of the car.

"Why do you need this? I hope you're not doing anything silly…." The text-to-voice audio from my speakers trailed off the farther away I went from my SUV.

I didn't even have time to lie to her. If I was going to catch Mason, I'd have to do it right now.

I did a quick scan for any other Broken Veins when I reached the bathroom door. There weren't any around. Tightly gripping the gun on my hip, hidden beneath my blazer, I took a deep breath and knocked on the door.

"Occupied" came the gravelly voice behind it.

I swallowed, then forced myself to proceed. "Sorry to bother you. I just… I dropped my wedding band in there. Can I please come in and look around for it?" My voice was both frantic and nervous, very little of which was acting.

*Calm down. He's just another fugitive,* I reminded myself.

"You dropped your wedding band in the *men's* bathroom?" As soon as the door opened, I pushed my way inside and then closed it tightly. I would need privacy for what came next.

"Not exactly." I smiled innocently.

Mason's eyes narrowed as he worked out if he'd

seen me before. It was irrational, I knew, but I felt a little wounded by that. How many girls did he pull that stunt with on the highway?

"You," he said, brushing his hair back. A slow smile crept across his rugged tan face. "White SUV?"

I smiled back slightly and dipped my head. "Yeah."

Mason Stone lived up to his namesake. His dark, sand-colored body looked rock hard. I fought the urge to run my fingers down his torso. I'd never seen any man in person who was in as good shape as he was. He was something out of a magazine.

"I take it you're not looking for a ring," Mason remarked, letting his eyes wander down my body as well.

"No." It was hard to keep my concentration.

"Then what can I do for you?" My heart rate spiked at the smokey tone of his question. It held so many implications.

I exhaled through gritted teeth. I was a little afraid. I also felt something else as well, something I hadn't felt in a very long time. It was an undeniable, primal attraction. Why did he have to be so damn handsome?

"I need you to put these on." I tossed him a pair of handcuffs. His expression went from sexy to surprised to amused. "Please?" I added coyly.

His smile widened. "Wish I could, love, but I'm—"

*You're here for a reason. Time to get to work.* I took another breath and steadied myself, then pulled my pistol on him. "I insist."

The mischievous smile bled from Mason's face. "Shit. What's all this?"

"Put them on." I clutched the gun tighter. "Now."

"All right, take it easy." Mason calmly snapped the restraints on both wrists, then held them up. "So, what are you? Statie, FBI, Marshal?"

I unsheathed the knife he kept on his hip and tossed it in the sink, then frisked him placing his cell phone and a few other effects into the sink as well. This collar was going to be hard enough to take in without giving him a chance to call anyone for rescue. If he had a gun, it was in his bike and not on his person.

I made sure to check him thoroughly. His skin was rough and hard and warm and wonderful. The manly way he smelled was all gunpowder, gravel, and fresh sweat.

*You don't have time for this*, I scolded, needing to stay focused.

"Let's go," I said, all business. We walked cautiously out into the parking lot.

"I might be a little rusty, but I seem to remember being read some Miranda rights last time I had metal bracelets on."

I opened the back door of my SUV. "Get in."

"You're not playing fair, lady." Mason was surprisingly unconcerned about the whole thing. He got in without complaint.

I pointed to a metal ring attached to the back of the passenger seat. It had an open keypad lock attached to it. When a fugitive was locked to it, they couldn't attack the driver. "Clip yourself."

"No. Not until you tell me *why* I'm being arrested."

I reached in and locked his handcuffs to the metal ring. "Oh, you're not being arrested."

Mason's unconcerned expression melted away. "Wait, what?"

"You will be arrested though, just not by me. I'm a bounty hunter."

"Oh, fuck," he said as some sort of realization set in. Why would he be more upset that I wasn't a cop? He then looked past me and spotted one of the other bikers. I tried to get out and slam his door in time. I failed.

"Spaz," Mason screamed.

The other biker searched around for a moment as I ran around to my side of the vehicle and jumped in. The Vein spotted us and shouted something back. I didn't catch it, but I'd guess it wasn't anything good for me. I turned the car on and hauled ass out of there. I was hoping I'd be able to slip away without the rest of his gang noticing. So much for that.

"You have no idea what you just did." Mason's deep voice rang out ominously. "Let me out right now, and I'll make sure they don't come after you."

"Thank you for your thoughts on the matter, but I'm going to need you to be quiet." Threats were nothing I hadn't heard a million times before.

"Those guys are fucking animals," Mason insisted. "They're going to catch up to you. When they do, I won't be able to stop them from what comes next."

"I don't need you to stop them." I addressed the audio connection on the Bluetooth. "Dial Nine-One-One."

"What are you—"

"Nine-One-One, what is your emergency?

I put on my best frantic voice and rambled. "Oh thank God! I just left the Plainview rest area, headed northbound, and-and-and I don't know if I cut one of them off or something, but I'm being chased by a biker gang!"

"Okay, ma'am, we have a unit nearby. Hang tight. What kind of vehicle are you driving—"

"Please hurry!" I tapped the button to end the call.

I could tell by the tone of his frustrated chuckle and snort that Mason was reluctantly impressed. "Crafty," he remarked bitterly.

I didn't bother hiding my smile. I was used to being underestimated. It was always that much more rewarding when I could show off just a little.

"Incoming call from… Kenneth," sounded from the car's speakers.

*Again?* A frustrated groan escaped me when I heard his name. Kenneth was incredibly persistent. It was great for capturing fugitives, but terrible when I didn't want to talk to him. I shook my head and was about to tell the Bluetooth to ignore it.

"Answer," said the voice in the back seat.

What? Had Mason seen my exasperation and deduced that I didn't want to talk to Kenneth?

"Eli?" Kenneth's familiar baritone rang out to unwelcome ears.

I shot a hateful glance through my rearview. Mason met it with a petty and smug smirk. He *had* done it on purpose, just to spite me.

My eyes shot past Mason through the back window toward the rumbling noise in the distance. The Broken Veins weaved in and out of traffic. They were gaining on me. I would have to end the call manually, but I decided I'd rather keep both hands on the wheel instead.

"Elisha," Kenneth called out again.

"This isn't a good time," I impatiently replied while pressing the gas pedal to the floor.

"I noticed the missing file. Please tell me you did not go after that biker scumbag and not tell me."

*Oh, you brazen sonofabitch.*

"That's how you're going to open this call? Seriously? I'd have called sooner, Kenneth, but I didn't have the number to Chelsea's pussy."

"Okay, yes, I'm sorry. I screwed up, Eli. I get it. I promise I'll make it up to you, okay?" Kenneth rattled off insincere apologies like he was reading the text from a pamphlet on placation. "You need to come home right now."

I laughed. I was done taking orders from a man who'd run out of second chances. Second? More like fourth or fifth.

"Dammit, Eli, listen to me. This isn't some strung-out druggie. You're in way over your head. You can't do this without me."

I don't know if he was attempting concern, but it came off like a challenge. For once he wouldn't be able to take all the credit. I narrowed my eyes. "Watch me, Kenneth."

"Oh, for…. At least tell me you're not alone."

I snapped another glance at the road behind me.

Cars slipped into the horizon, but the bikes kept getting closer. Even driving at top speed, I couldn't hope to outrun these guys for long.

*No, Kenneth, I'm certainly not alone.*

Anxiousness began to creep in, and my chest started to tighten.

"Hey, whoever you are, call the cops. Your girl kidnapped me. This is all just a big misunderstanding." Mason thrashed in the back seat. I wasn't worried about him, though. Not even a big guy like him could break his restraints.

"You caught him?" Kenneth asked, ignoring Mason.

I positively beamed at the sound of disbelief in his voice. He never thought I was capable of doing this on my own. After all this time of propping him up as the face of the company, it felt good to accomplish something this big by myself. He'd never be able to take that away from me.

It was the little victories that meant so much.

*Smash!*

My back window exploded inward, taking my smug smile with it. *My God, are they shooting at us?* No, but the Broken Veins had finally caught up. One of them was wielding a small metal pipe that looked like a tire iron.

I couldn't believe how fast they were.

"Was that glass? Eli?"

No words came out when I tried to speak. I found that I was having a lot of trouble breathing. *Oh no, not now!* I couldn't be having an asthma attack now. Not while doing ninety on the highway surrounded by men trying to kill me.

"Goddammit, Eli! Answer m—"

I punched wildly at the End Call button until I hit it. I had to get myself out of this, and I couldn't do that with Kenneth screaming at me. Even now, he'd found a way to make everything worse.

Then the wheezing started, and my airway constricted. I groped around the center console for the emergency inhaler that I always carried with me.

It wasn't there.

I could feel a fit of coughs rocketing up through my lungs and into my throat. I held my breath. If I succumbed to it, I wouldn't be able to keep my eyes open or stay on the road.

I frantically searched. It wasn't in the glove box or the door compartment. My vision began crackling around the edges. *Where is it?*

*Smash!*

My rear side window was destroyed too. I screamed out my last desperate gasp of air at the sound. A peppering of shattered glass tumbled over my shoulders. Bikers were on both sides of my SUV and edging closer to the driver side door. They were all over me.

The coughing crashed through me like a tidal wave of fists. There was no holding it back. I couldn't get enough air in my lungs to catch my breath.

*Oh my God. This is it....*

*My pocket!* I'd brought the inhaler with me to the rest stop bathroom. Patting down my sides, I found it. Shaking it, I popped the cap off and quickly inhaled. Within seconds I felt relief and could breathe again.

There was another impact, this time to the door on

my left. I looked over to see a crazy-eyed biker with a bush of a mustache staring back at me. He was terrifying, not due to his size but because of his intention. The grisly smile plastered across his face was one of extreme sadistic jubilation. He was a little boy with a magnifying glass, and I was the trapped ant.

I swerved, but they swerved with me. They were much better at this stuff than I was. I couldn't hope to outmaneuver them either. There was no place to run and no way to hide.

The glint of blue-and-red lights twinkled in my mirror, but they were so far away. I honestly didn't know if I could keep my vehicle on the road long enough for the police to reach us.

Just when I thought things couldn't get worse, I heard the familiar sound of a click in the back seat. It was the unlocking of the padlock that held Mason's cuffs in place.

*Oh no.*

That lock was my only defense from him climbing over the seat and attacking me. Mason's head rose into view in my mirror. I was completely helpless.

*My fugitive is free.*

I swerved again while fumbling to get my gun out. This was insane. What was I thinking? Kenneth was right; I couldn't possibly do this alone.

There would be no way for me to draw on him, aim, and fire before he got to me. I'd let my pride get the better of me, and now I was going to be strangled to death or stabbed or whatever.

I was such a fool.

Then there was another click, that of a seat belt latching itself together. Mason strapped himself in. He wasn't going to attack me for some reason.

"Jack on the brakes. Now!" Mason shouted.

Maybe it was the sincerity in his voice, but for some reason I listened and stomped on the brakes. The tires screamed louder than anything I'd ever heard before. My SUV started to fishtail, but I adjusted, then managed to keep the wheel as straight as possible.

I didn't know why I listened to him. Maybe it was because he could've killed me but chose not to. I couldn't begin to fathom what he was thinking. I was just glad to be alive.

The Broken Veins slowed down as well, but they just flew by. It was brilliant. Motorcycles weren't built for that; they didn't have the same braking power of a four-wheeled vehicle. A few seconds later, two state police cruisers blasted by me, and the Broken Veins had to choose between taking off and pulling over.

Either way, I had no intention of sticking around to see how it ended. My heart was pounding and my hands were shaking, but my asthma had died down.

Thank God.

What was I doing? I knew I should just wait here for more police to arrive and be done with it. I wouldn't be able to collect the bounty because I hadn't brought him to North Carolina. But so what? I was almost killed.

Then I remembered where I was and realized stopping for the police wasn't an option. Kentucky outlawed bounty hunting. Law enforcement were the only people here who could capture fugitives. Despite being commissioned by the state, I was no cop.

If I handed Mason over here, I could be in serious trouble. They could send me to jail.

"You all right?" my fugitive asked.

Getting my breathing under control, I responded. "I'm fine." I pulled my gun and aimed it through my seat at Mason. A dangerous man was still free in my SUV. "I'll be even better if I don't hear that seat belt unclick."

"It's Elisha, right? Let me go." The sincerity in Mason's voice was off-putting. "This is a world of shit that you don't want to be a part of."

It didn't matter if I believed him or not. Mason now knew who I was. Letting him go was appealing, but it was also now out of the question. He had enough info about me to be able to track me down or go after my loved ones. The only way I was releasing him was in cuffs to the authorities. And I couldn't do that here in Kentucky.

My only response was racking the slide on my gun, which put a round in the chamber, making the gun ready to fire. It was something my father always did with his gun; he said it prevented accidental discharge.

The sound stripped the remainder of hope from Mason's face. "So it's like that, huh?"

"It is." I did feel a little bad about it. I didn't know if it was just to save his own skin, but the advice he gave me probably saved my life.

He sighed and leaned his head back. "You're the boss."

I may have had my fugitive, but everything else was falling apart so fast now.

I took a hard left, driving over a patch of grass and through a thin wire fence. It was the only thing that served as the median between the north- and southbound lanes. Now back on the highway, going the opposite direction, I had to make a decision.

Should I go south to Tennessee, which was closer, and drop Mason off, or should I make the two-day drive east to North Carolina and collect the bounty? In any event, we'd have to hole up for the night at a motel.

And that came with its own obstacles.

# Chapter 2
## ELISHA

"Are these really necessary?" Mason sat on the closed toilet in the bathroom of the motel room I'd rented for the night. I locked his cuffed hand to the exposed metal pipe under the bathroom sink.

"Necessary? Asks the outlaw biker." I looked at him skeptically, then clarified. "Yes, yes, it is."

Mason rattled his wrists. "This borders on cruel and unusual."

"Well, so does nearly being run off the road by your psychopath biker friends. You can reach everything you need. You'll survive one night."

"I seem to remember saving your ass earlier."

I laughed at the absurdity. "You can't claim to save someone if it was you that caused the danger in the first place. If you hadn't called out to…." Slag? Spreg? The man's name eluded me. Biker nicknames were silly anyway. They never made any sense. "To whatever his name was, then my life wouldn't have been in danger to begin with."

"I didn't ask to be kidnapped."

"That brings us back to the part where you're a wanted fugitive." I made a circle gesture with my hand. "If it wasn't me, it would've been someone else."

I could see it on his face that Mason seemed troubled by that concept. How could he not know that people would be looking to bring him to jail?

"Can I at least make a phone call?" He looked up at me, his tone lightening. He gave me a hopeful smile and a shrug. "All things considered, it's a pretty reasonable request."

He was right. It was the decent thing to do. However, being all alone without the ability to even call the police myself if things went badly, I just couldn't take that chance. He'd have to wait till he was in a police station.

"No, I'm sorry." I shook my head. "I can't risk you calling your sadistic biker friends and telling them where we are. I get the feeling that wouldn't end well for me."

His lips tightened. It was a frown that held only bleak realization, as if he knew I'd say no. Or maybe it was because he knew exactly what the Broken Veins would do to me.

"No, it wouldn't." His tone was both mournful and ominous, almost like it was a forgone conclusion. The fact that it was so horrible that even Mason, a member of that gang, found it distasteful filled me with a chilling sense of dread.

I would not let the Broken Veins catch up with us.

"I won't call them. I need to check in with someone else, outside the club. I wouldn't beg if it wasn't important."

In my line of work, people lied to me constantly, so I'd gotten really good at sussing out the truth. I looked him over carefully. "Who? Who could possibly be so important?"

Mason started and then stopped, obviously struggling to find the right words. Eventually he just decided against it and leaned his head back against the cool tile wall.

"It's funny," he said, chuckling darkly. "I can't say. Not even to save my life."

He couldn't tell me? I found his clandestine reluctance a little amusing. He probably wanted to call his girlfriend or something.

"So you're a secret agent, then, huh? Can't have your cover blown? Y'know, I think I see it now." I squinted and scrunched up my face as if in heavy thought. "Clean you up a bit, throw a suit on you…." I whispered, "Are you James Bond?"

He chuckled, genuinely this time. "Careful." He tapped one of his rings, feigning seriousness. "This one shoots rockets. You shouldn't get too close."

"I'll keep that in mind." I stood up and turned to leave, then stopped. Something had been bothering me that I couldn't figure out. No one had ever broken free in my back seat before. Seeing his head rise up in the mirror scared the heck out of me. "Mason, how did you get out of that padlock earlier?"

Without tilting his head, Mason casually looked down his nose at me. "Must've kicked it just right when I was thrashing around back there. New lock, yeah?"

I couldn't remember exactly when I'd picked it up, but I knew it wasn't that old. Kenneth had just bought a pack of them; maybe he changed mine out too. He was always doing things without telling me.

I nodded.

"That happens sometimes. I read that about one in ten thousand are defective."

"Hmm, weird." How else could he have gotten out? It wasn't as if I'd dropped the key back there. Whatever, I'd just buy a new one the next chance I got. Besides, I had other things to worry about now. "I'll see if I can find you something to read, Mr. Bond."

Mason was out of luck, as the room only had an old Bible. I asked him if he was interested, but he declined. I couldn't put the TV on because I needed to be able to hear if he was trying to escape. This was a very precarious situation; I needed to be as cautious as possible, even if that meant it was going to be a long, boring night.

I'd brought my gun case in and laid out the cleaning supplies on the coffee table. With everything that was going on lately, my gun was overdue for a good cleaning. I set out a bunch of paper towels and began disassembling it.

I actually liked cleaning my gun. Oftentimes, I'd do both mine and Kenneth's after we went to the firing range. The mechanical nature of it relaxed me. They combined perfectly, and every small piece had a specific place. If anything was even the slightest bit off, then the whole thing would be useless.

My phone vibrated on the edge of the table, pulling me from my meditation. I could feel that it was Kenneth even before I checked to confirm. My hands were covered in gun oil, and a dozen small parts were carefully arranged on the table, waiting for me to reassemble them. He had a gift for calling at the least opportune time.

I let it go to voice mail.

The phone rang again. Then again. By the fourth call, I was sure he wasn't going to stop. I forced down the bitterness of his betrayal long enough to answer.

"What do you want, Kenneth?"

"Are you on your way back, Eli?"

I'd have rather taken the call outside, but I wasn't going to leave my gun in pieces on the table unsupervised either. I put him on speakerphone and closed the bathroom door for what little privacy I could manage. "You gave up your right to check in on me."

"Goddammit, Eli. I already apologized for that."

"And that somehow magically fixes everything? So what? It took me far longer than it should have to see you for what you are—a manipulative liar. There's nothing to apologize for, because there's nothing left to repair. We're done, Kenneth."

He sighed, sounding more annoyed than remorseful. "Then, as a coworker, I called to see if you were all right." I could almost see him pushing his tongue against the back of his teeth like he usually did when he was beating around the bush.

I glanced over to the alarm clock on the table and then pressed my eyes closed in disgust. Did he always lie this much when we were together, or was I that blind to it? "You waited seven hours to see if I'm all right? Just tell me what you want and stop wasting my time."

"Fine, I'll just say it, then. You're suspended."

"What?" The words hit me as if I'd walked out into traffic. I was the one who'd built our company from nothing. I was the one who'd spent countless long nights going over piles of legal paperwork, not him. He found us funding, but I did literally everything else. "We're partners. You have no right—"

"I've talked with my lawyer, and I do have the right. I know for a fact that you just checked into a motel in Kentucky with a known fugitive. We both know Kentucky doesn't like that. Right now, you're breaking the law, Eli. Our company bylaws say that if any partner is accused of illegal activity, then they are temporarily placed on leave until they can prove otherwise."

"You slimy piece of—" He must have gone through my bank records and saw that I used my card to buy the room. That was such a rookie mistake. I should've known better and just paid in cash.

"As of right now, you are no longer covered under the company's insurance or liability." It sounded like Kenneth was reading all of this off a paper.

"You are so petty, you know that? Instead of helping me through all of this, you're going to pull this on me? You make me sick."

"Don't project, Eli, okay? I'm just looking out for the good of the company."

"I built this business from the ground up, Kenneth. While you were out—"

The line went dead. The bastard had hung up on me.

My whole body tensed and shook as I stifled a scream. I riffled through my contacts, contemplating calling him back just to yell at him. I tapped the goofy, stupid picture I had for him in my phone. I needed to change that picture to something much less flattering.

I stopped the call right after I dialed.

What would that accomplish? He and I were finished in every sense of the word. These last few days had been some of the most taxing I'd ever been through.

I stared at the wall for some time and just fumed.

I realized that despite Kenneth being a massive jerk, he was partly right. From a legal standpoint, I'd pursued this contract completely on my own. If we had to fight it out in court, who knew how far that would go? I felt so stupid. Nearly everything we had was jointly owned. I could potentially lose everything.

What was I going to do? Tears came to my eyes, and I started to hyperventilate. Anxiety occasionally triggered my asthma. I became worried about having another attack, which only added to my stress.

My father came to mind. *Self-pity is a broken crutch. Get a hold of yourself, Elisha.* I thought of what he might say to me. He was the first black police officer in our town, and he was always my pillar of strength.

I focused on breathing and nothing else until my lungs began to relax. I was alone now; I had to be strong too. I missed him a whole lot.

Drying my eyes, I put my gun back together and tried to

busy my mind with the immediate. Live in the moment so as not to be crippled by the past or future.

The look that the mustachioed biker gave me earlier today came to mind right away. It sent a shiver up my spine. I'd never killed anyone before, and the thought that I might have to frightened me. The only thing that scared me more was what that psycho would do if he found me.

"Your boyfriend sounds like a real asshole" came Mason's surprisingly clear voice from the other room.

Gun in hand, I opened the bathroom door. He was still securely handcuffed to the pole, so I slid my gun into the holster I wore on my belt. "How much of that did you hear?"

"All of it." He shrugged dismissively. "This isn't exactly a bank vault."

"Wonderful. You must've loved that." I rubbed my brow. I knew I should've taken the call outside in my SUV.

"That's not the kind of thing that gets me off. It does sound like you're in a tight spot, though." I couldn't tell if it was genuine, but there was compassion in his voice.

I let out a defeated sigh, not wanting to say more for fear of looking weak. Weakness wasn't something I had the privilege of entertaining in front of my captives. Criminals would always take advantage of any opportunities you gave them.

"I do have a little experience on the 'tight spot' subject." Mason smiled, holding up his chained arm. "Kenneth was right about one thing. You're crazy to even attempt this by yourself."

"I caught you, didn't I?"

"Fair enough." Mason raised his eyes. "How much money are they paying for my ugly mug?"

It struck me that he was the first fugitive who'd ever asked me that. *Do I tell him?* It seemed like something I should keep to myself, but I couldn't really see why. If he told anyone else, then they'd just want to bring him in too. "You really want to know?"

"It's always nice to feel appreciated." He smirked.

"Okay." I shrugged. "Half a million."

"No shit?" Mason laughed. "And my high school guidance counselor said I'd never be worth anything."

I tried not to laugh, but it was no use. A giggle squeaked out of me. With all the uncertainty and hardship, it felt really good to laugh. I had forgotten the last time it happened.

"What do you say we both turn me in and split the money? When I bust out, I'll meet you on a tropical island somewhere."

"Tahiti does sound pretty good right about now. If you make it out of prison, I'll save you one of those fruity umbrella drinks." That was a delightful, if completely ridiculous, fantasy.

When the mirth finally started dying down, he asked, "Is the money the only reason you're doing this?"

"That much money? What do you think? There are certainly safer ways to meet tall, light, and handsome men."

A smooth smile spread across his lips. "So you do think I'm pretty?"

I started to blush. It was a poor choice of words. I'd meant it as a joke. Didn't I?

Even still, he was undeniably attractive. Rugged, strong, and in insanely good shape. I'd say he wasn't my type, but that was only because I'd never been around a man with all those qualities before.

He was definitely my type, minus the whole criminal thing.

Then he had to go and screw it up. "Who's Chelsea?"

My eyes flared at the thought of her. She'd slipped out of my head, but now she returned with a vengeance, dragging behind her all the images of her in bed with Kenneth. To think we'd started off as friends before I hired her. In retrospect, it was obvious. All the signs were there, I just chose not to see them.

"A woman who's soon to be unemployed." My voice seeped venom. "Our receptionist."

"Given a choice, I'd take you over her in a heartbeat."

I laughed. What a ridiculous statement. "You don't even know her. What if she's a supermodel?"

Mason scoffed. "I've never heard of a supermodel going toe-to-toe with one of this country's most notorious biker gangs *almost* single-handedly."

"So, is that your plan?" I smiled, raising my eyebrows. "Are you going to flatter me into letting you go?"

"That depends." He smiled back. "Is it working?"

I shook my head but couldn't hide the flushness that rushed to my face.

"If not that... I'm pretty good in the sack." Mischievousness returned to his eyes. It was the same look he'd given me at the rest stop.

*Oh really.* It was written all over my face. Quick, small sparks lit up throughout my lower stomach muscles. I felt my thighs tighten.

"You'll have to leave the cuffs on. I am a dangerous man, after all." His words pervaded my brain, coating it like chocolate-dipped vanilla ice cream. His tone threatened to melt me on the spot.

"Okay, Casanova," I teased him unconvincingly, attempting to change the subject. I didn't meet his eyes because I didn't want him to see how much he was affecting me. "Who's the wild-eyed biker with the mustache?"

"You buzzkill." Mason let his head loll back and grunted. "That ball of barbwire-wrapped hate is our chapter president, Double D. The way that guy smiles sometimes… I have to check to see if I'm bleeding after every conversation."

"I got that impression when he tried to smash my head in on the highway. You do keep some interesting company."

"If you want to call them that. Between him, Ginge the behemoth, and Spaz the coke-monkey, they'd put on one hell of a variety act. The murder and mayhem hour starring the Broken Veins." Mason couldn't get all the way through the sentence without chuckling. "Tune in, kids."

I laughed at the mental picture of the hard-core bikers balancing on a big red ball. Regaining my composure, I finally asked, "Why them?"

Mason gave me a confused glance.

"When I researched your file, I looked into your MC. Murder, racketeering, rape, coercion. Why did you join the Broken Veins?" I asked.

Mason held out his hands like he couldn't tell me anything.

I continued my line of reasoning anyway. "I get the whole camaraderie thing, I do, but there's so many other motorcycle clubs that have a much better reputation. Even one-percenters like Iron Hide and the Reapers aren't anywhere near as vicious. The Hells Angels and the Broken Veins' progenitor club, the Steel Veins, do charity work. "Yet you chose to join the worst of them? Why?"

"What makes you think I'm any better than they are?" Mason looked up at me, a flicker of penance in his eyes. "Maybe I deserve them."

I studied him. "I don't know."

I honestly didn't. It could've been the fact that he didn't attack me in the car or that he helped me to evade them on the highway. Or maybe it was just his demeanor and personality. Something about Mason made me believe he wasn't like them. "I've spent my professional life around the dregs of humanity. You're different somehow."

"Am I now?" He laughed. "What I am is *hungry*. Don't suppose this place has room service?"

I smiled at how quickly he changed the subject when I entertained the notion that he might not be all bad after all. That was fine. I didn't mind backing off.

"Judging by the color of the threadbare carpet out there, I wouldn't put money on it." Finding my feet, I stood up. "You don't mind muskrat, do you?"

"I'm more of an opossum man, but I've never been the picky type."

I took in his cracked, playful grin, then slipped out of the room.

It was really nice to talk and think about something other than my own mountain of problems. Mason was handsome and funny and deceptively smart. I had to wonder if the Broken Veins had something on him. There was more to this story—more to him—than he let on.

Could they have forced him to join?

I also realized that it didn't matter what his story was. I had my own, and they definitely didn't dovetail together. For one of us to get what we wanted, the other couldn't. And if I didn't finish what I'd started, then I lost everything.

Mason had a checkered past, but he didn't seem all that bad. Maybe in another life, we could've played a game together that wasn't cops and robbers. I felt a fluttering in my chest that reminded me that I was a woman first and a bounty hunter second.

There wasn't much to eat in the area. Across the street was a convenience store that had an attached deli. The deli was closed, but I was able to grab a few sandwiches that were left over.

Through the constant din of legal issues, worry, and anger, whenever I thought of Mason, I found myself softly smiling. It was crazy, and I chased it away immediately every time, but try as I might, I couldn't completely get rid of the feeling. I wasn't sure that I even wanted to.

On my way back to the room, I realized that, with two broken windows, I couldn't leave anything of value in the SUV. I grabbed my duffel bag from the trunk and checked the back seat. When I opened the door, a small sliver of metal on the floor caught the motel's exterior lighting and twinkled.

At first, I didn't know what the thin, bent, and jagged piece of metal was, but when I picked it up and studied it, I felt extremely stupid. It was a lock pick. Of course. The lock wasn't defective—Mason picked it.

He lied.

I scolded myself for giving him the benefit of the doubt. He was a damn criminal! My father was probably rolling over in his grave at the fool I had been. It was all there in the file. He was a car thief originally; it wasn't much of leap to think he knew how to pick locks too.

I unlocked our room's door. Without breaking stride, I tossed everything on the floor, drew my gun, and kicked open the bathroom door. Mason was testing his cuffs, but it didn't look like he'd gotten them off yet. His right hand was still attached to the pipe.

"Faulty lock, huh?" I got lucky. If he had called someone… I didn't want to think about that.

"Take it easy." He rose from the toilet and raised his hands. "If I hadn't found a way to put on that seat belt, I would've lawn-darted through the front window when you jacked on your brakes to get away from my MC."

"Oh, and that was a little detail you overlooked when we talked earlier." I squinted at him as I adjusted the grip on my gun. "So, what was the plan? You gonna wait till I fall asleep and pop your bonds? Then what? Smother me with a pillow and steal my car?"

"You've read my file. I don't do that shit."

"But you were going to take my SUV, weren't you?"

Mason looked at me hard but didn't say anything.

"Yeah, that's what I thought." I shook my head.

"This is all a mistake. I can't be here, Elisha. There's something much bigger going on than some backwater, misfiled paperwork bullshit."

I was done believing his lies. I should never have allowed myself to open up to him in the first place. He'd played me like a foolish lonely girl. He probably had a lot of practice with that. Well, I was fed up with all of it. It was time to start doing things smarter.

"Strip," I demanded, tossing the cuff keys on the floor near him. "I want all of it."

He started to crack a smile "You're joking."

"You heard me," I said with a steely resolve. My tone was all business. I refused to be fooled again if he had another lock pick stashed away in his sock or wherever. This was the only way I'd know for sure.

I expected more protests, but Mason stayed quiet after that. He wasn't ashamed or hesitant. He locked eyes with me, daring me to blink as he unlocked his hand and slowly peeled each layer away.

First was his cut, the vest he wore that was covered in his MC's patches. Grabbing the sides, he rolled it off his shoulders. The muscles in his chest, neck, and arms rippled with fluidity before the heavy leather slapped against the tiles.

That was when I noticed the massive burn running up

his side. It ran almost parallel to the tribal snake tattoo he had on the opposite side. I wanted to ask him about it, but now definitely wasn't the time.

Then came his reinforced denim riding pants. They had no zipper, only buttons, and with every one he popped open, he searched my eyes for a reaction. I really needed to swallow, but I resisted. I refused to give in, to show him that this was something other than necessary.

Mason flayed out the fly, hinting at the formfitting gray cotton of his boxers underneath. He hooked the waistband of his jeans with his pinkies and dragged the thick fabric down. My eyes flicked over him, searching for more lock picks that might have been stashed away. That's what I told myself.

His legs were steel cables under white skin that hadn't seen the sun in a while. That did nothing to slow the swell of urges that were surging within me at the sight of all his naked flesh.

My breathing spiked when I caught sight of the massive outline that ran down his leg. It would've been a lie to say that I hadn't thought of him like this. Even still, his cock was a lot longer and thicker than I'd been prepared for. A cotton barrier was the only thing between us. My face flared with heat.

He stood back up, sliding his free hand over his scalp to get his chin-length hair out of his face. Mason's eyes were black orbs in the harsh, humming light. Impossible to read. They pierced right through me, not with malice or disdain but with something else. Something that made my pulse race.

I'd removed my jacket earlier but was still wearing everything else. Somehow, when he looked at me like that, I felt like I was the one who was standing there naked. The way he carried himself, there was a starkness about him. Truth laid bare. Mason exuded confidence, even now.

I began to speak, but the words were lodged in my throat. I swallowed them and started again "All of it," I said finally, as evenly as possible.

"Take them down yourself," he dared me.

Mason wore an air of defiance, clearly testing how far I was willing to go. Would I cave and show him that my threats were meaningless? Would I start, then get too overcome with embarrassment and stop?

"Fine." He'd gotten it all wrong. I wasn't timid or sheepish. I motioned for him to lock his hand back up. He did.

Gun clutched tightly in hand, I curled my fingers into the waistband of his boxer-briefs and began to tug. The fabric stretched and slid over his hip bones, exposing the trunk of his thick shaft.

I wasn't afraid I wouldn't be able to continue.

I was worried that I couldn't stop.

I breathed him in so deeply that his scent had seeped into my pores. His cock tunneled beneath the cotton as it swelled and lengthened. It launched my heart into my throat and made it pound like a jackhammer. It was hard to think, to process.

*What am I doing?* screamed a distant voice. *Stop!*

Maybe it was the adrenaline in the situation. I didn't want to admit it, but God, I wanted to feel all of him. I'd only slept with a few men, and none of them came close to making me yearn as badly as Mason. I snapped my eyes back up, capturing his no-longer-passive stare. Now his intentions were loud and clear.

He wanted me too.

The frustration of clarity finally rang out like a sharp warning bell striking at night's end. I was kneeling down before a near-stripped fugitive who I was bringing to custody. I may have started out looking for hidden items and weapons, but whatever I was doing now wasn't that. My emotions were all over the place.

I abruptly let go of everything but the gun, then leaned back. It didn't matter what I wanted. I was a professional.

*I'm in control.*

Mason's body lurched forward after me in nothing but his boxers. The metal cuff whined against the pipe, preventing him from following. Seeing the pipe flex filled me with worry and also a little excitement. Would it even stop him if he decided to continue what we'd started?

Mason stepped back, letting the chain relax. For a moment I just watched the rise and fall of his rib cage. He was breathing heavily as well. I holstered my gun and locked eyes with him one last time. Neither of us knew what to say, or even if there was anything left to say. I'd still need to check his clothes for anything that might let him escape, so I grabbed the bundle and left.

I dropped his clothes in a heap on the bed and quickly

rifled through his pockets. There was another pick hidden in a pack of cigarettes, but nothing else I could find. I was still pissed at him for lying, but what did I expect? I'd probably do the same thing too if I were in his situation.

He'd get his clothes back in the morning. It was a really warm night, and the AC was broken in the motel room, so I wasn't worried about him getting cold. I'd even be sleeping on top of the comforter tonight.

God, I was such a wreck. I lay down on the bed and rubbed my eyes. Single for barely a few days, and here I was swooning over the very definition of the 'wrong guy.' Still, I couldn't get Mason out of my head.

What if I'd gone through with it? I would've been vulnerable enough for him to take advantage of me. I knew it was wrong, but the thought of his rough, strong arms manhandling me flushed my cheeks with fire.

I hadn't felt the dull drag of my nails at first. Not until they grazed the band of exposed skin between the bottom of my shirt and the elastic of my panties. My lower stomach was hot to the touch, transporting my mind back into that bathroom where I'd stood only inches away from Mason, his hard body radiating heat like a hell-bent furnace.

My teeth dug into my lip as I quietly worked the button on my suit pants. I listened with bated breath to the near-silent separation of metal teeth in what was the longest unzipping of my life. The whole time, with the walls as thin as they were, I prayed that Mason couldn't hear it.

My conviction wavered with the rapid beating of my heart. I knew my prayer was a flimsy thing, easily trodden on by an all-consuming lust. A part of me hoped Mason heard every subtle click of the zipper.

Sliding my pants down, I stopped and listened for sounds coming from the bathroom. Nothing. Was Mason asleep already? Or was he at rapt attention, deciphering every noise I made and replaying it in his mind?

I knew I shouldn't, but I continued anyway. Kenneth and I hadn't had sex in months, and when we did, it was boring and unsatisfying. Not to mention too quick. We'd lost what little spark we'd had after all these years.

Mason's presence alone was white-hot lightning, and because I'd drifted too close to it, my body cried out for release.

I focused on my fingers as they slid between the wet lips of my pussy, imagining they were his. My touch was rough and foreign and exploratory, as I hoped his would be. I could almost feel the heat of his trapped cock on my face as I threatened its release.

I closed my eyes to send my imagination back into that room with Mason and his bulging cock. I had no tolerance for being teased. Licking my finger, I slid it in and wiggled it just the way I liked it. I wanted to feel the way my supple flesh would yield to the coarseness of his stubble as it scratched its way across me.

When my second finger invaded me, I moaned. It was faint but audible. I couldn't find it in me to care. My legs flexed and stretched as they kicked Mason's pants from the bed. I pushed my palm into my clit, sending a pulse through my limbs. I was getting close.

With my free hand, I reached blindly to squeeze something, anything. My fingers grazed the oiled, smooth leather of Mason's vest. Without thought, I grabbed it and pulled it over top of me. I breathed in as deeply as my wounded lungs would allow. Its distinct and manly musk sent my head swimming.

My chest crushed in as I came. I gritted my teeth to stifle the moan. One hand smoothed tight circles over my clit while the other pushed Mason's leather into my pussy. I needed its roughness against me more than I needed air in my lungs or blood in my veins. God, I loved the pressure.

Several ragged breaths later, I lay there with my eyes still clamped shut. The climax had done little to curb my craving for Mason, but at least it relaxed me enough that sleep would be a little easier tonight.

I opened my eyes when I realized that I'd left the bathroom door open. I half expected him to be standing over me, but he wasn't. I had mixed feelings about that. Eventually I decided it was good that he wasn't.

A quiet exhale escaped from the other room. It was the sound that accompanied a knowing smirk or a satisfied glance. Even with all the lights off, it was lighter in the motel room than I'd realized. With darkness and lust stripped away, embarrassment welled within me.

*Oh my God,* I thought, no longer as cavalier as I was a few minutes before.

*I think Mason heard me.*

# Chapter 3
## MASON

Elisha made her way across the parking lot back to the SUV with a plastic bag full of snacks and food. It was only in the honest morning sunlight that I was able to see the cool tones in her rich brown skin. It was a beautiful shade of twilight afterglow. I didn't think it was possible for her to get prettier, but this woman was nothing if not full of surprises.

Her black hair was pulled back into a tight bun, still smoothed from her morning shower. She had on a gray blazer over a soft purple button-up shirt that was tucked into gray suit pants.

As she opened the SUV door, she met my gaze with no hesitance. There was a vulnerability in her deep brown eyes that said she was worried about being in over her head, though it was carefully guarded behind confidence, cunning, and a steely reserve. She seemed like the kind of person who was plagued with a dogged tenacity. Come hell or high water, she'd see her goals to the end.

That didn't bode well for me.

She wore ruthless professionalism easier than most

women wore perfume. The Elisha who left the motel with me this morning was much different than the one from last night. She was colder, more resolved. She'd made it abundantly clear what our roles were.

I couldn't blame her. After what we almost did, I could understand why she would try to distance herself from me emotionally. If that was the case, I hoped she was doing a better job at it than I was.

All the shit I'd gotten into with my club, the law, and the meeting with Ratchet buzzed around my head like mosquitoes I couldn't swat. It was heavy, life-altering stuff, and yet here I was, locked in the back seat, tracing Elisha's curves and aching to finish what we'd started.

Last night had not gone at all according to plan. I needed to escape, and the few times I might have been able to overpower her felt too wrong. I was smart enough to find a way out of this without harming her; I just needed to figure that out. Whatever I was going to do, I needed to do it fast because I was running out of time, and so far Elisha had seen through my every attempt.

Almost.

Last night while she was out, I was able to pick my cuffs and make a very important call. Not to my club, of course. If they caught up to us, they would kill Elisha. That was if she was lucky. Who knew what Double D would have done to her?

I couldn't have that resting on my conscience.

The sign welcoming us to North Carolina blurred past. Stretching my neck, I could just barely make out the time on her dashboard clock.

"We're not going to make it before they close," I said. Small-town police stations closed surprisingly early.

"Yes, we are." The SUV abruptly pulled forward as she stomped down on the gas pedal.

"I bet you I'm right. Call ahead if you don't believe me. If they're open, you won't hear my voice the rest of the ride."

Elisha pulled out her phone and scrolled for the right number. She called, putting the phone to her ear, having disabled the Bluetooth feature after I answered the phone call from Kenneth. I was still feeling pretty smug about that one.

As it was ringing, she begrudgingly asked, "And if they're closed?"

She'd been so cold the whole ride that I didn't think she'd even entertain the bet.

"If I win, you let me go."

She laughed, sharp but genuine. "Not likely."

"Just a kiss, then."

She turned her head to hide her smile, probably not wanting to break whatever restrictions she put on herself. She couldn't lie to me the same way she could lie to herself. It was impossible and insane, but the connection was there. The attraction wasn't right or just, and considering what our situations were, we damn well shouldn't act on it.

Despite the performance she put on, I could see that part of her knew it too. There was a war waging in her mind and heart. Elisha was torn between what she should do and what she wanted to do.

Consideration for consequences had never stopped me before, especially if it was something I wanted. I knew I should be focusing on getting to the meeting with Ratchet. My life literally depended on it.

Ratchet was just another member like me. He didn't hold any office within the hierarchy of the club, or even have any responsibilities within his own chapter. What he did have was the big gun cartels on speed dial. He was the main connection between the Broken Veins and millions of dollars in gunrunning money.

He was unofficially one of the most powerful members in the club, and for some reason he wanted to see me. Come hell or high water, that wasn't a meeting I could afford to miss.

All the shit with the Broken Veins loomed over my head like a tidal wave, and yet all I could think about was her. I couldn't tell if Elisha was a lifeboat or an anchor, but I sure as hell wanted to find out.

After several fruitless calls and more miles than I could remember, we reached my old stomping grounds. Carver, North Carolina. There were some good memories, but far more that I'd like to forget. It'd been at least a decade since I'd lived here, and that wasn't nearly long enough.

"I was right, wasn't I?" I had to keep my mind occupied. Nostalgia wasn't friendly to me here.

Elisha ignored me, pulling into Lucky's gas station and convenience store. I used to steal candy bars from here when I was a kid. Putting the SUV in Park, she replied, "We're stopping for the night. I'll grab us some dinner."

It had gotten warm enough that she stripped off her jacket and tossed it on the passenger seat before heading into the store. I watched her walk into the store and couldn't take my eyes off her. Something about Elisha was so damn refreshing.

I'd been with a lot of girls before, but none were like her.

Elisha stopped, bending at the waist to tie a loose shoe. The gray cotton pulled taut against her tight ass. She knew I was watching. She had to know. Did she do that just for my benefit?

My cock bulged at the teasing promise. After last night, I needed to touch her. To run my hands down her silky skin. Maybe that was the real reason I hadn't escaped by now. If that was the case, then I was truly out of my mind.

What was I thinking? How could one woman be worth two years of dangerous work? I couldn't really be risking everything just for a piece of ass, could I?

In the several minutes that Elisha was inside, I let my posture and my gaze lower. The last thing I wanted was for someone in my past to recognize me. That wasn't a conversation I was looking forward to having. If anyone saw me chained up back here, word would spread, and then my deal with the feds would be compromised.

On the floor by my feet, I spotted another one of my lock picks. I'd dropped a bunch when we were being chased by the Broken Veins and just assumed Elisha found them all. I picked up the tiny sliver of metal and slid it into my sock.

I'd escape tonight after she fell asleep.

Elisha exited the store with a bag of groceries in one

hand and a six-pack of beer in the other.

"No shit?" A beer was *exactly* what I needed right now.

My relief faltered. There was a growing weight settling in my chest. The thought of leaving her at whichever motel we stopped at bothered me for some reason. She hadn't told me exactly what was going on with her ex-boyfriend, but I could read between the lines.

She was up against a wall, and the money she thought she was going to make off my bounty was the only thing giving her hope.

It was almost a shame that there wasn't any actual money waiting for her, even if she did manage to bring me in. I couldn't tell her that, of course, not without royally fucking myself over.

I just wished there was a way I could convince her without jeopardizing myself in the process.

"I take it that's my consolation prize?" I asked when she opened the door.

"You think this is for you?" Her words were thick with skepticism as she started the SUV. "What makes you think this isn't for me when I bring you in tomorrow?" She threw an arm around the passenger seat and craned her head back toward me so she could look out the rear window and back up.

"Keep the beer," I said, trying for eye contact. "I was after something much sweeter than that anyhow."

Until I did escape, what was wrong with having a little fun?

Elisha's eyes brightened and her face began to flush.

She didn't dare match my stare, swinging around in her seat and using her mirrors to back up instead.

"I never agreed to the terms of your bet," she said defiantly.

I could hear the resolve in her voice waver as she sped off.

I knew where Elisha was headed for the night. There was only one motel in the area, the Mashdaw Inn. The last time I was back in town, it was a shitty, run-down wreck; I could only imagine the shape it was in these days. The only people who ever used it were out-of-towners who had to spend the night for court, dropouts who needed a place to shoot up, or locals looking to screw around on their spouses.

It had the familiar end-of-the-road desperation I remembered when we pulled up, but there was obviously work being done to it. Half the rooms were closed for renovation. Was Lou, the guy who owned it, finally going legit?

Lou still lived in a retrofitted double suite at the front of the long rectangle of a building. It was attached to a small one-room office that had windows on three sides. As long as the money was good, Lou never asked questions. He even made it a point to keep poor records. It was the perfect place to stay if you didn't want to be found.

The room was in better condition than I'd expected. The interior had been redone since I came here with my friends all those years ago. There was new carpeting, a flat-screen TV, a queen-sized bed in the middle of the room, a kitchen nook with an oven, the whole nine yards.

It wasn't high end by any means. There was still an obsolete radiator in the back corner of the room that needed to be removed, and as nice as the new bathroom was, I still didn't want to sleep in it. The soft carpet was luxury in contrast.

"If you're going to lock me up again, can you do it out here? Another night on a tile floor and I'm going to gnaw my arm off."

Elisha thought about it, then eventually complied, cuffing me to the unused heater. "Please don't make me regret this." She handed me the six-pack.

"It's no umbrella drink in Tahiti, but it'll do." I twisted the cap off a beer and handed it to her first. She declined. I snorted when I realized they were all for me. She must have thought if I was drunk I'd be less likely, or at least less capable, of sneaking away.

Beautiful and cunning. I couldn't help but be impressed.

"Don't tell me you're going to make me drink alone?" I put a beer on the end table by the bed for her and opened another. "You might as well chain me back up in the bathroom while you're at it, Warden."

"Someone as crafty as you?" She turned away. "I think you'll do just fine in prison."

"Admit it. You're going to miss me when I'm gone."

Her phone began to vibrate.

"Not even a little," she lied, then checked the phone. Her softening playful features went immediately rigid. The expression on her face turned to one of dour anger. I didn't need to see the phone to know it was Kenneth calling.

Elisha took the call outside. This time I couldn't hear what they were talking about, but I could hear the tone at which they were doing it. It was several minutes of silence, then bouts of screaming, followed by more silence.

I couldn't imagine how blind or stupid Kenneth had to be to fuck up so badly with a woman of her caliber. If I were in a better place and I knew someone who was half as smart, driven, and gorgeous as Elisha, I wouldn't have stopped until she was mine.

Elisha came back inside composed, but her eyes were red and puffy from crying. She snatched the beer I'd opened for her and drained almost half of it in one go.

"Everything all right?"

"No," she said between sips, then chuckled to herself weakly. "Everything is not all right." Elisha sat on the bed, just out of reach, and slowly rubbed her face. "I think about how many years—" Her words choked off. It was hard seeing her so distraught. I felt like I needed to say something, but I was never very good at consoling people.

"There was a girl I chased all through my teens and early adulthood," I started. I didn't presume to know what she was going through, but I could at least offer her a distraction. "This girl threw me for a loop. She knew exactly how to play me with the perfect mix of flirtation and elusiveness. This was all way back before I'd ever heard of motorcycle clubs."

Elisha wiped her eyes and looked at me, patiently listening.

It was a painful story, one I'd tried desperately to forget.

Being back in Carver made the memory excruciatingly vivid. The scars worn on the inside always ran the deepest. With our forced proximity, Elisha had no choice but to show me the emotional scars Kenneth gave her. The least I could do was show her one of mine.

I looked through the far wall like it was a window into the past.

"I'd fallen so damn hard that there was nothing she could do or say that would shake me. She had this deep, amazing smile that was utterly hypnotizing. When I looked at her, I was the only man in the world. She'd kiss me one night, then fuck one of my friends the next. She led me on like that for years, and, like a fool, I followed. I was too blinded by what I wanted her to be that I never let myself see who she really was until it was too late."

"When did it become too late?" Elisha asked, her grief giving way to interest, mixed with a hint of concern.

"When she finally said yes." I smirked darkly, looking back at Elisha. "It was almost a year before I realized that I hadn't married the fantasy version of Kate, the one I'd made up in my head so long ago. When she eventually left me for someone else, it was a shock to no one but me.

"Through all the pain and anger, I was glad that it happened the way it did. I learned a lot about myself from her. That still didn't stop me from making a shitload of mistakes. Obviously." I chuckled, holding up my chained arm. "But at least now I know what kind of man I am." My smirk lightened, becoming just an honest smile. "And what kind of woman I actually want."

"I'm sorry to hear that." Elisha averted her gaze. "The file didn't say anything about you being married. When did you really see her for the first time?"

"When she had the kitchen painted sea foam green." I shook my head distantly, ruminating over the memory. "It was then that I realized I didn't know her at all. Who does that to an innocent kitchen?"

"Are you playing with me?" Elisha clearly wanted to laugh but stifled herself.

"Only a little. I made her return the paint before it was too late. Everything else is true, though."

"Okay, good." Elisha laughed, then caught herself and apologized. "That came out wrong. I'm sorry. I know how hard all of that is."

I gave her a knowing look and nodded.

Finishing my beer, I popped open another and offered it to her. "I'm willing to bet that there's a lot about me that's missing in your file."

"Yeah? Like what?" She was still nursing the half a beer she had and waved off my offer.

"Well," I said, thinking it over, "does it say anything about me playing piano?"

"It does not." There was jovial surprise in her tone.

I leaned in and spoke softly. "That's because I don't play piano."

"Come on," Elisha protested, but I could see she was having fun.

"But"—I put my hand out in a calming gesture—"I do play violin."

Elisha eyed me. "Seriously?"

"Since I was nine. As you can tell, I was super popular in high school."

Elisha seemed taken aback. She studied me, trying to discern if I was telling the truth or not. "Violin, huh? I just—you don't come off as a violinist."

"Is it because I'm white?" I said it as straight-faced as I could.

"What? That doesn't even make any sense." She laughed and reached for her second beer. "It's just that you're the first outlaw biker I've ever even heard of that plays. Are you any good?"

It was nice to hear her talk candidly, even if she did mean to have me arrested. At least I always knew where I stood with Elisha. There were no nagging suspicions that she might screw me over. She was very clear about her intentions.

"I'm a little rusty now, but I'm sure I can still bust out 'Amazing Grace' with the best of them."

"Well, then." Her face turned in an impressed mock frown.

"I know this great little music store downtown. Let's blow off the whole court thing tomorrow, and I'll show you what a lowly biker really can do."

Elisha's mood fell. She sighed.

"Mason, you know I can't. If I didn't need the money as badly as I do… I don't know. I shouldn't be talking to you this way. And I definitely should not be drinking." She swirled her beer around and cocked her head in a dismissive gesture.

"All this is only going to make things more difficult."

I could've steered the conversation further down that direction, but I didn't want to. I couldn't remember the last time I'd had a meaningful discussion with someone who wasn't either trying to use me or test me. Pretending to be someone you weren't was exhausting. When I was around Elisha, I felt like I could put down the many faces I wore to survive and just relax.

Elisha got up to put some physical distance between us. Maybe she wanted to clear her head.

"Wait." I stopped her. "You're right. I'll cool it with that. I'm just looking for a way to pass the time."

"Okay." She took a deep breath, exhaled, and sat back down. "But I'll hold you to that."

I figured she was craving a conversation that didn't end in yelling and heartbreak as well. I still had no idea how I was going to get out of this whole thing, but I knew I wasn't willing to hurt her and steal her SUV. Whatever my options were, they'd be tomorrow's problem.

"You know all about me and my deep, dark, musical secret. Tell me a little about you."

"Me?" The subject change put her on her heels. It was clear that she hadn't thought she'd be on the receiving end.

"Is there someone else here?" I asked, watching her smile. "Has your asthma always been that bad? You were in rough shape for a while there."

"Usually it's pretty mild. It takes a lot of stress for it to really flare up on me. Unfortunately, stress doesn't seem to be in short supply these days. Between Kenneth, the business, and your lunatic friends—" She raised her eyebrows at me accusingly before letting them drop and continuing. "—it seems like my stress levels have recently gone through the roof."

She pulled her inhaler from her pocket and turned it over in her hand. "But as long as I keep this on me, I should be all right." She took another sip. By the way she drank more easily, I could tell she was beginning to relax.

"Should you be drinking if you're asthmatic?"

"Probably not." She smiled mischievously, pressing the bottle to her full, rich lips.

Goddamn, was I envious of that beer.

"Well, cheers to bad decisions, then." I held out my beer, and she clinked it with hers.

Elisha slid off the bed and sat next to me, the mostly empty six-pack between us. "I never did get the chance to thank you for your help getting away from the rest of the Broken Veins."

I let her words linger before responding. My eyes narrowed on her intently. "You could repay me with that kiss."

*No way she goes for that,* I thought. Even still, I wasn't the type to let an opportunity fly by. Elisha didn't say anything, just ever-so slightly bit her bottom lip. Desire threatened to overcome her better judgment.

Instinctively, I moved to caress the side of her face, but didn't even make it halfway before my cuff snapped taut.

"That's your fault," I said with feigned indignation. I laughed, looking up at her through raised eyebrows.

"Yes, it is." Elisha smirked in amusement then to my massive disappointment, she suddenly stopped and pulled away. I fell forward after her until I could catch myself. She let out a long sigh then put some physical distance between us and sat on the bed. Running her hands over her face she composed herself. "That would be very unprofessional. Regardless of all the other crap going on there's just some lines I can't cross. Beer is one thing but..."

Elisha's breathing was rapid and shallow. I could see that she wanted this too but wasn't able to find peace with allowing herself to indulge. Getting herself comfortable on the bed she emptied her pockets onto the nightstand beside it. I had a feeling she wasn't going to allow herself to get any closer to the criminal on the floor. It was too dangerous in every way that wasn't life threatening.

"Professionalism is key." I half chuckled half snorted the words out. That's when I noticed my heart was racing a little. Something about the way she carried herself and how unwavering she was in her commitments, while shitty for me at the moment, was really admirable. "From one troublemaker to another."

Elisha smiled at that.

We were so caught up in leaving the world outside behind that neither of us heard our room's door slowly unlock.

Two Broken Veins burst in.

The ugly, harsh world had finally caught up. Our moment had passed.

We were fucked.

# Chapter 4
## MASON

"You're Cowboy, right?" asked the first Vein. He was an older, wide man who wore a bandanna to cover his receding salt-and-pepper hairline. He had a graying beard that was cut and styled into a point and was long enough to graze his belly. Gun drawn, he lumbered into the room. He had the impatience of a tired grizzly bear that was reminded of the coming winter and was eager to wrap up the hunt.

The second Vein was all sinew in comparison, with a pallid jaundiced complexion. With short-cropped hair that was roughly the same length all over his body, he looked like a shaved, elongated weasel. His twitchy and jerky movements suggested that he was either ramping up on or coming down from something nasty. PCP maybe?

They both wore the same vest as me. The only difference was their patches were from a local North Carolina chapter.

"Yeah," I said, standing up, hoping to draw attention away from the woman who was hiding on my side of the bed. Elisha had excellent instincts, and knowing that any uninvited guests would be trouble she rolled to relative safety at the first sign of noise at the door. Even still with how fast everything had happened I couldn't be positive they didn't see her so I played dumb and tried to distract them as best I could. "Did my chapter send you?"

"Yap," the bear said with a sigh. "I'm Gunner. This here's Gintin. Where's that bounty hunter who's got you all locked up?"

"You didn't have to come get me. I've got everything under control."

"Control, huh? That why you're chained up like a dog? Or is it some whips and chains dungeon shit." Gunner raised an eyebrow. "You ain't one of them faggot Cowboys from *Brokeback*?"

There was a tense moment between us. Clearly Gunner wasn't what anyone would call progressive.

"I'm just fucking with you." He laughed uproariously and began to walk over. "Ain't no faggots in the Broken Veins. You're just lucky I had to wait for Gintin's release from county. Otherwise, I'd be headed to the meet m'self."

Elisha had quietly reached for her gun that fell off the bed earlier but was spotted.

Before I could answer, the twitchy one fired a shot at the foot of the bed. It punched through comforter and linens. I recoiled from the noise. Elisha screamed and jerked her hand back toward her.

"C'mon out," Gunner barked, rubbing his ear at the loudness. He shot an angry glance at Gintin for firing too close and hurting his ears. "Stand up, girly. Don't make us come fishin'." Gunner was growing more impatient.

I nodded to her. Elisha's eyes were upturned in worry, but only for a moment. She steadied her breathing and buried her concern under a facade of sternness. She wouldn't let them feed off her fear. My admiration for her instantly doubled. She nodded back, then stood up.

"Naw shit, look at that. We got the black tittied bitch here too!" Gintin energetically exclaimed. "You snappin' offa piece of that chocolate bar?"

It was only then that I spotted the flat black swastika tattooed on the side of his neck. I'd seen enough stick jobs to know he got that tattoo while in prison. That was going to make getting Elisha out unscathed much, much harder.

"I'd ask if you're all right, but..." Gunner lewdly sniffed the air and laughed. His massive stomach heaved up and down. It didn't matter that we hadn't actually done anything, a man like him of course would just assume we had.

"This is all a big fuckup, Gunner. You didn't have to come all this way." I kept my eye on Gintin. He circled around the bed and blindly kicked Elisha's gun into the kitchen somewhere. His mouth hung open slightly as his eyes trailed over every inch of Elisha's body as if she were standing there completely naked. I tried to step between them, but I was still chained to the goddamn wall. "My girl and I were just having a little fun. I had an errand in Carver, and then we were headed to the annual ourselves."

"Don't tell me you got that Stockholm bullshit?" Gunner eyed me suspiciously. "We know all about this bitch. One of your guys had her license plate run, found out she was a bounty hunter. I'm gonna let your pres know

we found ya. Gintin, get those fuckin' things offa him."
Gunner dismissively waved in the direction of my cuffs,
then turned away to talk on the phone.

Gintin snapped his grubby fingers at Elisha, but she
jerked away before he was able to get any real purchase.

"Hey!" Elisha hissed.

"I'm just looking for the key, that's all." Gintin's tone
was defensive as he squeezed his cock through his jeans.
With the wiggling fingers on his other hand, he tickled at
the covered nook between her thighs. Elisha moved back,
obviously wanting no part of him. She slapped his hand
away. "Never know where they hide them. Might have to
do a thorough examin—"

"It's on the key ring on the nightstand," I interrupted
coldly. I could only force down so much anger. Some of it
boiled out into my tone anyway. "Hurry the fuck up."

I had to be smart about this. *Put that outlaw mask back
on*, I reminded myself. *Be one of them just a little longer.* I
couldn't afford to fly off the handle. Not yet, not until I was
free, at least. Attached to the radiator like this, I couldn't do
shit to help Elisha.

I needed to get free.

"My bad, bro." Gintin snickered, slipping away. "You
northern boys keep some strange company." Soon he had
the key ring in his hands and was jingling the keys in the air
set to a tune I didn't know. He went to toss them to me, but
Gunner stopped him. While still on the phone, he caught
Gintin's arm and held up a finger telling him to wait.

Gunner hung up after a beat, then looked at me for a long

while before speaking. It was the same way my last judge looked at me right before he told me what my sentence was going to be. "The Philly chapter is on their way. Double D wants you to stay put. Says he found your phone and has a few questions for you."

*Fuck. They must have grabbed it from the bathroom at that rest stop.* I thought hard about my call history and how I named my contacts. One in particular worried me. If they found out who I'd been talking to, they'd gut me alive.

"And the girl?" Gintin's nasally voice pulled me out of my contemplation. I couldn't worry about later when Elisha needed me now. She pushed herself against me, and I wrapped my free arm around her. I wanted to put her behind me, but that just wasn't possible. We were pushed against a corner.

There was literally nowhere for her to retreat to.

Gunner raised a disapproving eyebrow at Gintin, one born more of racism than ethics. Seeing his wiry counterpart's hopeful gleam, Gunner shook his head and shrugged. "Whatever. Gotta kill her anyways."

Gintin let go of his cock and eagerly reached for her.

"No!" Elisha yelled defiantly, making Gintin have to work at it. She slapped his hand away again and flailed when he tried for her arms.

With lightning precision and force, I wrapped my free hand around Gintin's throat. His eyes bulged as I squeezed. Even one-handed I was more than a match for him.

"That'll be enougha that." Gunny had his gun trained on me. When I didn't budge, he shifted his aim to Elisha instead. I had to let go.

Gintin gasped when I released him. He staggered away, then returned more cautiously, vileness in his eyes. "I can do her alive or dead. Don't bother me. Her body'll stay warm till I finish either way. I won't need long."

I could feel her pulse begin to race and hear her breathing become more shallow and rapid. Elisha dropped her arms and pulled away from me. I grabbed her hand.

"No," I whispered to her. I said it again, louder, firmer.

She peeled my hand off her and walked toward the human weasel. I flexed against my bonds. I knew I wasn't walking out of here, but I refused to believe I couldn't help her.

Even if that meant tearing my own hand off to do it.

Gintin grabbed her by the bun in her hair and jerked her head back. "It's been so long...." The words oozed out of him.

"I can't fucking watch this. I'm headed out for a smoke." Gunner shook his head in disgust. He probably wouldn't have allowed it at all if he didn't know she'd be killed afterwards.

Gintin stopped his slobbering and shoved Elisha into the chair by the door. A look of embarrassment crept across his dull features. "Gunny, you know that I don't go for the dark meat, right?" He reached into his pants and casually adjusted his cock while appealing to his friend. "It's just been a long time, and... I mean, fuck! I'm horny enough to fuck anything right now. You know that, right, Gunny?"

Gunner just waved him off and let the door slam

behind him.

"Fuck. Don't go tellin' no one I'm a nigger-fucker!" Gintin yelled through the closed door to Gunner. Pissed off but undeterred, Gintin turned back to Elisha. "Desperate times call—"

The sentence was smashed out of the human weasel's mouth by the alarm clock Elisha had ripped out of the wall. The biker staggered, eventually tripping over his own feet and falling into the opposite wall.

Elisha dropped the clock and lunged for her keys that had been left on the entertainment center. She scooped them up and threw them to me. While in midthrow, Gintin grabbed her ankle and wrenched her to the ground. The toss went extremely wide, and the keys landed uselessly out of reach.

*Fuck!*

"Elisha!" The word escaped me as I watched her fall. The bureau rocked from where her head impacted it on the way to the floor. Dazed, she lay there as Gintin rolled her onto her back. Her forehead was split open and started bleeding. I couldn't tell how bad it was.

"Hey! It's Gintin, right?" His head stupidly rotated to look at me. "Listen, man. You've been in prison awhile, and I know you're fiending for drugs and pussy and all that. So, from one Vein to another…."

He'd already lost interest and started turning back around.

"If you don't back up right now"—my thinly veiled appeal was pushed aside by my mounting frustration and rising anger—"I'm going to put my thumbs through your fucking eyes. You hear me, you weaselly little prick?"

Gunner loudly rapped his knuckles against the room's large front window. He couldn't see in due to the blinds being drawn. "The fuck is all the racket in there? You all right?"

"Bitch just likes it rough is all," was Gintin's only response.

"For fuck's sake…. Move that shit along, would you?" Gunner walked off.

"You heard the man." Gintin moaned. "Sorry, bro. She's club property now."

I couldn't fucking stand it anymore. It felt like I was being torn apart. Blood was streaming down my wrist from straining against the cuff. I grabbed the radiator with both hands and put every ounce of my strength into pulling. The metal strained, the wood creaked, but the radiator wouldn't budge.

Gintin had a hand on her throat, strangling her while he wrestled to get her pants down.

"Get the fuck off me!" Elisha cried out between labored breathing. I saw the vibrant, wonderful color in her face wilt like a plucked flower on a car's dashboard in early August. She called out again, but I could no longer hear the words.

"Mason." I read my name on her lips. I watched the hope fade from her eyes as her heavy lids threatened to close forever.

*The lock pick!*

I reached for my socks and emptied the pick onto the carpet. My fingers were slick with sweat and blood, but I worked at the cuff feverishly. Picking lefty was much harder for me; it required both calm and patience, neither of which I had.

The lock clicked. It was almost free when my only pick snapped in half. My last hope to get to her was gone.

Frustration and rage blinded me.

All I saw was red.

*No.*

I turned back to the radiator and renewed my pull. This time I was too angry to stop. I'd tear hell out of the ground or rip myself apart trying.

Long cracks in the painted Sheetrock walls spiderwebbed out from the radiator. The tremendous strain made the veins ripple along my flexed forearms. Brimstone ignited within me, setting my blood on fire at what he was trying to do to her. I was filled with rage-fueled clarity of purpose.

I growled with exertion like nothing I'd ever felt before.

*I refuse to let this happen.*

"Enough," I muttered. A loud pop came from the wall.

I ripped the cast-iron heater off its mounting and jerked it through the air. Filthy rust-colored water flooded the room, splashing everything. I collapsed on top of the radiator a few feet away.

I'd done it! I was still stuck to the radiator but was no longer attached to the wall. My muscles were Jell-O from the force it took me to get this far. They threatened to fail me altogether.

Gintin was so singularly focused that he was oblivious to what I was doing. He still had his gun, and he was too close to getting what he wanted to stop now. He had his cock out and was desperately trying to get Elisha's pants down past her knees. As disoriented as she was, she still made him fight for it.

"Enough," I said again. My voice boomed, not with volume but with definitive authority. Crackling red strength surged through my limbs. Squatting deep, I hefted the radiator and charged him.

I hadn't known Elisha long, but it didn't matter. I would rip that small man in half before I let him touch her a moment longer. And there wasn't a force on earth that could stop me.

"Goddammit!" Gintin squealed, looking up at me. Having no choice but to break away, he fired a few shots at me.

The radiator in front of me deflected each round. Nearly five hundred pounds of angry muscle and rusted metal crashed into Gintin, plowing his upper body into the carpet.

His head caved in like a smashed watermelon. Bloody bits of bone fragments and brain matter splattered me through the spaces between the pressed metal fins. His limbs convulsed with abandon for several seconds before falling still.

All that was left of him was a chunky red smear on the ruined carpet.

Elisha gasped for air. There was no relief for her even after Gintin's hands were removed from her throat. I rolled onto my back and reached for her. She was already gone, crawling for the inhaler she kept in her jacket's breast pocket. She breathed in the medicine like a drowning woman who'd finally surfaced.

"The keys. Hurry!" I called out to her. Gunner was just outside; he'd be in any second now. Rough sex or not, it was typically over when gunshots were fired.

I rooted around for Gintin's pistol. My arms were numb, but I knew I couldn't stop. I was fairly certain the gun was beneath either him or the radiator. If that was the case, there'd be no way I could get it in time.

I heard Elisha scramble for the keys, but it was too late.

The door was kicked open. The ornery Vein darkened the doorway, surveying the gruesome scene in utter disgust. Not at the bloodshed. That was a mainstay of the outlaw MC life; it always seemed to get messy. It was his friend's deadly incompetence that astounded and disgusted the man—Gintin couldn't even kill one black bitch?

Exhausted, all I could do was lie there and watch Gunner raise his gun. I stirred, hoping he'd shoot me first. Maybe I could buy Elisha some time to escape or fight back. A part of me knew it was only wishful thinking.

He had us both dead to rights.

When the gunshots sounded, I wasn't hit, so I immediately thought the worst. My heart broke at the thought of Elisha's lifeless body hitting the floor.

That was until the gun slipped from Gunner's hand. He fell to his knees, clutching at the glowing red circles on his stomach and chest. He'd been clipped in the heart and was spraying blood between clenched fingers. He was dead by the time his face hit the carpet.

Elisha stood rigidly with the smoking gun clenched in her shaking hands.

Her image was striking. She was sweating, several of the buttons on her shirt were gone, and blood ran down the side of her determined face. Fierce and strong, Elisha reminded me of a picture I'd seen once. It was a darkened bronze sculpture of Gorgo, the warrior queen of ancient Sparta.

I'd never seen anything more beautiful.

"Are you all right? Were you hit?" I asked.

"Jesus Christ!" she exclaimed, dropping the gun.

The statue began to falter. The adrenaline had started to wear off, and her cough and hard breathing had returned. Between Gintin and Gunny, few people had been tested like she had just been. When her back was against the wall and her instincts kicked in for fight or flight, Elisha was all fight. She now knew what she was made of.

She blew me away. I couldn't think of another person I'd rather have in my corner than her.

Elisha finally got me the keys so I could get the damn cuffs off. My wrist was all torn up and would need some attention, but that would have to wait till later. We weren't out of the woods yet. The Philly chapter was on their way, and I had no idea when they were going to show up.

What I did know was we could not be here when they arrived.

Between my club and my other obligation, I was in a world of shit.

My eyes drifted over to Gunner, now facedown in the corner. I thought I was saving Elisha. I'd gotten it so twisted. I'd be dead now if it wasn't for her.

"Elisha, breathe. Come here." I reached for her. She took

my hand and hugged me. It took several minutes for her crying to subside and for her asthma to calm down.

"You're going to be all right," I whispered to her. "I promise."

# Chapter 5
## ELISHA

I had just killed a man.

Gunner was a bad man who was going to kill us. I understood the necessity of it, but knowing the why didn't shake the way I felt. It was horrible. It was nothing like target practice or using a Taser on someone.

The permanence of firing my gun rattled me.

"It was them or us, Elisha. Remember that." Mason's tone was flat and hardened. He wore a mask of grim stoicism. If this sort of thing bothered him, he didn't show it.

Was that just for my benefit? I glanced at the gore stain that used to be Gintin's head. The brutality of it made me shake.

Or was Mason more dangerous than I'd come to think?

"Okay." It took a Herculean effort to leave the warmth and safety of Mason's arms. I'd never felt more protected in my life than I did with his arms wrapped around me.

Dangerous or not, Mason stopped the unthinkable from happening. My skin hadn't yet stopped crawling from that foul man's touch. Past the conflicted emotions, I was glad

Gintin had been put down like the rabid animal he was.

We both gathered our things and headed out to my SUV to find we wouldn't get far in that, even if we did take it. My tires were mutilated. No doubt that was what Gunner was doing outside when he let that animal try to rape me.

*Oh God… more are coming.* Who knew how far away Mason's MC was. I couldn't go through that again, not this soon. My anxiety started to flare up.

Being afraid of the coming Broken Veins didn't slow them down any, so I pushed through the fear and began walking toward the small office at the front of the building. "We need another vehicle. Maybe the owner can—"

"Wait." Mason grabbed my arm and looked past me.

I followed his gaze and gasped. A body on the floor prevented the office door from closing. I could see from here that it was the man I'd booked the room with. He was surrounded by a pool of dark liquid.

"We're going to have to take one of the bikes," Mason said, leading us back to our motel room.

"What about the police?"

"What about them? The station is closed till tomorrow morning, remember?"

*Shit.* He was right. That's why we stayed here in the first place

"The only thing that matters now is that we survive tonight." Mason rifled through Gunner's pockets, then Gintin's, taking whatever money he could find and a set of keys. "I know a spot back toward Kentucky where we can crash for the night. In the morning, I can take you to a place where you can call the police, or catch a taxi. Whatever you want."

"Wait a minute." This was all happening too fast. I needed time to think. Time to breathe. Everything was spiraling out of control.

"We can't hang around here, Elisha." Mason sat on one of the motorcycles. He tried the first set of keys. When it didn't work, he tossed them and tried the second set. They slid right in. "C'mon, hop on."

"No." I drew my gun but couldn't force myself to aim it at him. Not yet.

He paused. I was nearly as surprised as he was. "Elisha…."

After all of this, I couldn't just let him drop me off somewhere and disappear. I was too close. "I'm sorry, Mason. We're not going back the way we came. I need this too much. Tomorrow morning, we're coming back here and going to the police station."

Mason stayed quiet and eyed me. It wasn't the glaring stare of betrayal I expected. That, I could've handled. It was one of disappointment. I was compelled to continue, to explain myself more. I was swallowing daggers.

"Mason, I appreciate what you did for me, but this was always what was going to happen." Every word I said stung me as I heard it. My heart screamed and ached in vile protest. "Nothing has changed."

That was a lie.

I was walking a razor's edge with how close I was letting myself get to him. He'd saved my life twice now from the very people who were trying to rescue him. He wasn't like any bounty I'd ever dealt with before. If I was being honest with myself, he wasn't like anyone I'd ever known before.

I had to weigh my naïve and ridiculously inappropriate feelings for him over every other aspect of my life that was worth saving. I needed that money for a lawyer and for a fresh start. Maybe I could somehow even help Mason with it. Pay for a better lawyer for him as well.

The one thing I did know with absolute surety was that if I didn't bring Mason in tomorrow, Kenneth would squeeze me out of the business. My house, my livelihood, everything I'd ever known would eventually be wiped out with the stroke of a pen.

I liked Mason. Far more than any sane person should in this situation, but in the grand scheme of things, we'd only known each other a few days. What were a few days in the span of an entire lifetime?

Mason sighed, shaking his head. He was quiet for a long time. I could tell he was fighting bitterly with something difficult.

"Fuck," he growled to himself, obviously realizing I wasn't going to change my mind. He reached into his waistband and removed what looked like a thick USB memory stick.

I had searched him. Where did he get that?

I began to ask him what that was, but he held a hand up to stop me. Mason looked it over as if he was making sure of something. That's when I realized it wasn't a memory stick at all. It was a small recording device.

*What the hell?*

"This is an audio recorder. It was given to me by my handler in the FBI. This hardass piece of shit, Agent Harris."

"The FBI?" Since when did a biker need a handler in the FBI? Unless… "No, you can't be."

Mason chewed on the inside of his cheek before grunting out the words I was desperately hoping not to hear.

"I'm an informant," he said through gritted teeth. "A rat for the FBI. There is no money. There never was."

"You have to be lying. I saw the file. I even called to check." I lowered my gun, my stomach twisting with anxiety.

"Fucking Carver. Of course they would fuck this up. It was a misfile that was never removed from their system. You ever wonder why the amount was so high for such a small offense?"

"No…." I felt it all begin to unravel. "No. That money *has* to be there. Kenneth told me he's going to file to take my company from me. I need that money!"

I was so singularly focused that I'd ignored all the other signs, just like I did with Kenneth. Dammit!

"It's not there," Mason appealed to me in his gruff way. "If you bring me in, they're going to arrest you for interfering with an undercover operation. Even if they don't press charges against you, they'll at least hold you until this sting I'm on is over. I have no idea how long that'll be."

"Why didn't you tell me before? Why did you let me come this far?" Anger bubbled up in me. I didn't know how, or even by who, really, but I felt an overwhelming sense of betrayal.

Like I was some cosmic joke.

"Because telling you the truth would've…." Again, it took him a while to reply. "No. Telling you *has* blown my cover. If Harris finds out what I just said, they'll cut me loose on the spot. I'll head back to prison, and if I go back now, I'm a dead man."

*Jesus.* It was too much to process. My eyes started to water. I didn't sign up for any of this. This was supposed to be my way out, and now everything was a mess. *What have I gotten myself into?*

"Everything I know about you is a lie. I bet you don't even play the violin." He began to speak, but I cut him off. "What did you do that was so terrible?"

"We don't have time to dig into that right now. But I can prove it to you."

"I don't know what to believe."

Mason got off the bike and started toward me.

"Stop." I raised my gun at him. He pressed on like it wasn't even there. My hands started shaking. "Don't make me shoot you. You know I can."

He only stopped when my gun pushed against his chest. He grabbed the barrel and slid it over his heart. If I pulled the trigger right now, there was no way he could survive. I felt sick. There was no fiber of my being that wanted to hurt him, but I didn't know if I could trust him. He was a professional liar.

What choice did I have?

"I'm not the bad guy. But the real bad guys are coming. My cover and my life are now in your hands, Elisha. So either you shoot me, or you get on the back of that bike. Either way you need to decide right now. What's it going to be?"

Mason wasn't trying to intimidate. If anything, there was a little fear in his eyes. It wasn't fear of what I was going to do to him but what they would do to me. That terrified me. I knew right then that I would never have shot him.

I lowered the gun. The armor I wore around my heart cracked and fell away. Tears streamed down my face. I didn't even try to hide it this time. Mason thumbed them away and kissed me on the forehead.

He almost tore his own arm off to save me from that biker psycho inside. As horrible as everything was, there was a small, growing part of me that desperately wanted it. To ride off with him and never look back. To put this shit life behind me.

Mason extended his hand.

I was already at the bottom. What more did I have to lose?

I put my hand in his and let him lead me back to the motorcycle. With every step it felt like my grasp on the life I'd lived was loosening. How much longer before everything I'd ever known was swept away forever?

What scared me was that I was alarmingly all right with it.

God help me.

I was going with Mason Stone.

# Chapter 6
## ELISHA

I woke up in a cold sweat. The sound of a gunshot rattled through me like a coin in an empty soda can. My mind and heart raced as I snapped open my eyes and looked around. I expected to find the filthy hands of those bikers grasping at me. I threw my arms out defensively, flailing for my gun on the nightstand.

It was just a dream.

There was no gunshot, I realized. Gun in hand, I fell back into the bed and tried to calm my frayed nerves. *That's another thing,* I thought, gripping my gun tightly. *I still have my gun.* At any point while I slept, he could've taken it from me, but he didn't.

Why?

All the blurry details slowly came into focus when I let my eyes take in the daylight-soaked room.

Every wooden surface in the room was covered in doilies, stuffed animals, and clutter. The bed had too many covers and decorative pillows to be practical. This room could've been in a painting depicting picturesque white

American life in the fifties.

It also had the air of a mini mausoleum for a very young child.

It chilled me to the core.

The whole house had that museum exhibit feel to it. Despite all the smiling porcelain dolls, there was a palpable sadness to it all. This couldn't be Mason's house, could it? Where were we exactly?

Mason only told me it was a family member's house. I'd have asked more, but our priority at the time was getting the hell out of that motel before the rest of his club arrived.

I shivered when I spotted the reddish-brown dots up my forearms. It was Gintin's blood from when I fought him off. My head began to pound from where I'd fallen and hit the bureau. I'd cleaned the blood off my face, but the small cut had still scabbed over. It was tender to the touch, but I didn't think it needed stitches.

I laid out my clean clothes, then walked into the bathroom and stripped down. What I did need was a shower, and I needed it immediately. The blood on my skin began to burn into my soul like acid. I couldn't wait for the water to warm up before getting in. The eventual hot water washed away much of the horror and hardship. It also did wonders to soothe my waves of guilt, anger, and fear.

When had everything become so uncertain?

I'd left the window open, so the rest of the bathroom was cool and clear. When I finally stepped out, I felt like a real person again. I stood there naked, watching the steam sizzle off my skin, and just tried to breathe.

I wiped the fog from the mirror to look myself over for cuts and scrapes I might have missed.

My hair tickled the top of my shoulder blades. I briefly contemplated doing something else with it, then just sighed and put it in the usual tight bun. It had been such a long time since I wore it any other way. I didn't know when it happened, but at some point I stopped trying new things.

I hugged myself, smooshing my modest breasts. My skin looked especially dark and foreign amidst the cream-colored walls and the bright animal knickknacks that held hand soap and toothbrushes.

I felt so out of place here. I wanted to go home.

But where was home for me? My house or the office? No, that was all tainted by Kenneth. Where did I belong now?

The only time I was even remotely at ease was in Mason's arms. I didn't belong there either, but at least I was protected. I felt like I could let my guard down, just for a moment. If home was safety and warmth, then that was the closest I'd felt in a long time.

It was funny in a sad way. The closest thing I had to comfort was in the arms of a criminal who I was determined to bring to justice.

I finished dressing and eventually found Mason in the garage. After seeing the rest of the house, I'd have thought the garage would be just another storage area. I was expecting a few dust-covered cars that hadn't been moved in a decade or a pile of furniture and trinkets.

That was not the case at all.

The first thing that hit me was the smell. This was a man's playground. Oil, sawdust, and sweat. The garage door was open, but it didn't do much to dissipate the noxious fumes of the spray paint Mason was using.

The garage was carefully organized and taken care of. It abounded with life and activity as if it was the only part of the building the owner used.

Mason was bare to his waist and glistening in the morning sun. Every part of him was a chiseled masterpiece, a tan-painted marble sculpture given life. His hair was slicked back beneath a bandanna and sunglasses. Grease, oil, and paint were smeared up his powerful arms. From the looks of it, he'd been out here working on the stolen bike for a while.

Was it stolen if the man it belonged to was dead? Gunny's dying image rushed me again. It was so damn hard to shake.

Every time I squared off my target on a firing range, I'd imagine what it'd be like to actually kill a man. I always thought I'd be prepared for it. I was very wrong. The bloody gurgling, the writhing, the last gasping breaths...

Nothing can prepare you for it.

The worst part of it for me was how easy it was. It took more effort to open a pickle jar than it did to pull that trigger.

*"It was them or us, Elisha."*

Mason's words from earlier soothed me. Of course, he was right. The longer I watched him, the more my pain and guilt melted away. As hard as it was to pull that trigger and kill that man, I was still glad I did it.

I had no other choice.

"Shit got crazy. I had to get the hell out of there," Mason

said, pacing back and forth.

I'd been so lost in my own head that I didn't realize he was on the phone.

I leaned back away from the doorframe, hiding but making sure I could still hear him. Terror tightened around my chest like a vise until my breath was slowly squeezed out.

What if he told them where we were?

What if they were already on their way?

"No, I didn't kill Gintin and Gunner! I was chained to a fucking wall. I might have been able to help them if *you* had let Gunner free me." Mason lied with a convincing protest, then listened to what must have been more accusations. "Who the fuck do you think? Fucking Steel Veins rolled in there like a goddamn wrecking crew. Had to be five of them." Pause. "How the hell should I know? Maybe the motel owner called them. Carver is their turf."

Mason took his sunglasses off and ran a hand over his face and head. This was another side of him that I'd only seen briefly. The hardass MC thug, full of piss and vinegar. What I couldn't understand was *why* he would lie to them.

What bigger game was he playing?

Every time I thought I had him pegged, I was completely wrong. It was infuriating. He had so many layers that I had no idea who the real Mason Stone was. How could I possibly believe a man like him?

It was his own gang that he saved me from. That was a hard fact to gloss over.

"When they killed Gunner, I took his bike and got the

fuck out of there. I'm in some dive near the Tennessee border. You want me to wait for you?" Mason asked.

There was a pause just long enough for my heart to lodge itself in my throat. If they were coming, would I still have time to take him back to the police station in Carver, or should I just run for my life?

"Okay, I'll meet you at the annual, then."

*Oh, thank God!* I put a hand to my chest and sighed in relief. I couldn't go through that again. At least not so soon.

What exactly was his plan here? Butter me up with stories of his past and then sic his gang on me, hoping to escape in the chaos? But then again, he saved me from them when he could've just looked away. Then there was all that stuff about being an undercover informant for the government.

Everything was so complicated. Nothing made sense anymore.

"The girl?" Mason asked. "I thought I was getting a quick blowjob. The next thing I know I was stuffed in an SUV and—" Pause. "Where is she now?"

My heart stopped again.

"Dead," he said gravely. "Gintin brought her out into the woods somewhere and killed her."

The starkness of his words and his matter-of-fact tone shook me. Gintin *could* have done just that. I hadn't thought about just how close he'd gotten. It made my head swim.

Mason changed the subject with a smooth casualness. "Gunner said you had some questions for me."

There was a quick silence.

"Whatever you say, Pres." Mason sounded as if he

were coupling the sentence with a shrug. His unconcerned demeanor fell away when he hung the phone on its wall mount. There was a low growl in the back of his throat as he hurled a wrench across the room.

I jumped back at the sound of the crash. By the time I poked my head back out, he'd already gone back to what he was doing before the phone call.

There was a sense of resignation about him, as if he was used to shouldering this amount of stress. I didn't know if I should be frightened or impressed. I just wish I knew more about him. Just being around him had been a roller-coaster ride of emotions.

I stood there a while longer, noiselessly watching Mason. With quick, powerful bursts, he maneuvered bike parts around like they were a toddler's toys. It was the rhythm of a man venting frustration.

Or raging against the inevitable, whatever that might be for a man like him.

Mason had painted everything a glossy black. Between that and the new license plates he had on the floor, I knew what he was up to. He was altering the bike enough that he could use it and not worry about being pulled over by the cops.

The bandage on his wounded wrist was still raw and filthy. I could see him favoring it when he hefted the gas tank. He either didn't care about the pain or refused to let it slow him down.

Mason was strong in a way I was never surrounded by growing up. Where my father's strength was in his moral resolve and firm beliefs, Mason's was more primal.

His capacity for violence scared the hell out of me.

Mason was an all-consuming flame that skirted the edges of control. The thought of him ripping that radiator out of the wall and crushing that psycho beneath it sent a chill rippling through me.

With that much strength and control, I shuddered to think what might happen if he really let loose. Would I be around when that stray spark turned Mason into a full-on forest fire?

His voice suddenly boomed, startling me again. "You going to just stand there and watch me?"

How long had he known I was there?

"No," I said, recovering my composure. "I'm debating on whether to shoot you or not."

"You are one hell of a shot." He mounted the gas tank on the bike and bolted it back on. There was no playfulness in his tone, not like before over beers. Had his facade finally dropped? Was this the real Mason Stone?

I was hesitant on how to proceed. From the call, it didn't sound like we were in danger, at least not at the moment, so I tested the waters with some small talk. "Did you sleep at all?"

"There's plenty of time for that when I'm dead." His reply was slabbed granite, cold and hard. "How much of that did you hear while you were eavesdropping?"

"Enough," I said, not backing down. "You told them I was dead." My hand rested on the handle of the gun I wore on my waist.

He looked at it. "If I wanted to kill you, I'd have done it while you slept."

That was hardly reassuring. A shiver crept up my spine.

"Why did you tell them that?" I asked.

"You still don't get it, do you? Who do you think you're fucking with here?"

I didn't respond.

"If they knew you were alive after what you did?" Mason continued. "Abducting a member. *Killing* a member. These are the Broken Veins. Our members top nearly every list the FBI has, everything from America's Most Wanted and violent crimes to domestic terrorism."

He was right. Most of the sites I'd used to research the club were run by the FBI. I was so scattered at the time with everything that was going on with Kenneth that I just needed to get away. Maybe if I thought about how dangerous the motorcycle gang was with a clear head, I wouldn't have taken Mason's contract.

"Being dead is the only way you're going to survive this." He spoke with what sounded like honesty, but I didn't know if I could ever be sure again.

"How long do I have to be dead for?"

"Until tomorrow night. After my meeting with Ratchet, you can run for president for all I care. Nothing will matter after that." The notes of sadness in his voice made me feel pangs of sympathy.

Why? Why should I feel anything for him? What if he was playing me like he just did to his own club? God, the man was such a mystery. It was infuriating.

"Why should I believe anything you say?" I narrowed my eyes, sticking to my conviction. "Give me one good reason why I shouldn't drag you back to Carver, collect my reward, and be done with you and this whole twisted nightmare."

"You make it extremely difficult to keep you alive, you know that?" Mason walked back to the phone.

"What are you doing?" I instinctively went for my gun. What if he'd changed his mind and was going to tell his MC that I was still alive and where to find me? I couldn't take that chance.

"Putting all the cards on the table. You don't believe anything I say? Can't blame you. Guess I'll just have to prove it to you." Mason eyed me, gritting his teeth. He dialed a phone number, and as the line started to ring, he waved me over to listen to the conversation and added, "Stay as quiet as a church mouse. If the person I'm about to talk to even suspects I'm not alone—"

After the call went through the voice on the other end of the phone asked, "Who's this?"

"Harris, it's me," Mason replied, turning the receiver out so that I could hear better.

"About fucking time. Your shithead biker friends called me with your phone."

Mason paused, his eyes flashing wide for a moment. "What'd you tell them?"

"I told them I was your sick uncle, and that I was slowly dying of some horrible, barely pronounceable illness. That should cover your call history." Harris stopped, hearing

Mason sigh with relief. "I just got a disturbing report dropped on my desk. Did you have anything to do with that fucking horror show at the Carver motel last night?"

"Carver, North Carolina? I heard about that. No, that wasn't me." The lie rolled off his tongue with ease. Mason had obviously become very good at it while working undercover.

"So for the record, you're telling me you don't know anything about a bounty hunter's SUV being in that motel parking lot?" There was a deliberate pause from Harris. It was a thinly veiled accusation if I'd ever heard one. "The parking lot in *your* hometown."

I was glad I'd called to report my SUV as stolen. If he was talking to the FBI, it could be really bad if they found out I was actually there in person.

"I try to avoid most bounty hunters." Mason glanced back at me. "They tend to be nothing but trouble."

"Well." There was a pause on the other end. Whoever was speaking was clearly weighing Mason's words, trying to decipher if they were true. "It's a goddamn shit show here because of it. The new director thought it might be tied to that terrorist attack the other day."

"Terrorist attack?"

"For fuck's sake. Turn the news on every once in a while, shithead," the irritated voice barked at Mason, then switched gears. "Where's my audio stick?"

"Dropped it in the mail this morning. You should get it soon." Mason held his tongue.

"I'd better considering how you didn't leave it where you

were supposed to."

"I tried but I couldn't get away from the MC long enough," Mason said. "Lately they've been on me like white on rice."

"More like flies on shit," the man on the phone shot back. "Where are you now?"

"I'm at my house."

This was his house? How many secret lives did Mason lead? Who was this guy?

"You want to tell me what in the hell you're doing there? You should be in Arkansas by now for that annual!" Harris quickly worked himself up into a lather. I imagined spittle spraying out of the receiver at Mason.

"I needed to water the plants."

"Real fucking funny, wiseass. You, like my shitty cracked coffee cup, are government property. Don't you forget that."

"How could I? You remind me every time we talk." Mason spat the words back at the man.

"Don't fuck with me, Stone. What time is the meeting?"

"Five o'clock at the farm."

To pick up the new recorder, Harris only told Mason a combination code and the name of a city—Memphis. They must have some finely tuned system in place, because Mason quickly acknowledged that he understood.

Memphis. Was that where he was headed for the night?

"If anything goes wrong and you don't get me what I want, I will *personally* shit all over your WITSEC interview. You fuck this up and you will be crushed under the full weight of federal law. This is your last and only chance to avoid prison. You understand me, Mason?"

"Yeah. Loud and clear." Mason replied slowly and evenly, with a tone as grave as a funeral march.

"Get yourself another cell phone. And for fuck's sake, don't lose it this time." Harris abruptly hung up.

Mason was telling the truth about everything. The weight of that blow struck with enough force to physically push me back a step. All that work was now meaningless. My dreams and hopes were gone.

I felt inwardly naked, as if everything had been stripped away from me.

The hard facts I'd relied so heavily on turned to smoke. Technically, as long as he was working with the feds, he was no longer a fugitive, or even a criminal. At least not at the moment. I thought back to all the trouble with his club, the close calls and near deaths. It was all for nothing. We were just a man and a woman in a dirty garage.

Mason replaced the phone on the wall mount and turned to me.

"Satisfied?" he asked.

No, I wasn't satisfied. I was crushed.

Fully holstering my gun, I slumped down to a sitting position on the stairs. With my elbows on my knees, I covered my face. Mason didn't try to console me. I wouldn't have either if I were him. I kidnapped him, threatened everything he'd been working toward…

And for what?

I felt horrible.

After several earth-shattering minutes of contemplation,

I finally collected myself enough to look up at him. Mason was leaning on a workbench, his gaze a million miles away. The carefree version of him that I first met in the bathroom of that rest stop was a distant memory. Every layer of him I peeled off held another secret, another variation of Mason.

"Who are you?" I asked.

"Just a man who's paying for his mistakes." His eyes refocused on me.

I wondered if I was another of those mistakes to him. If he could have gone back, would he have let his club kill me?

That felt wrong even as I thought it.

"What happens now?" I was numb.

"You're staying with me until the meeting," he responded, cold and quick.

"What? No!" The Broken Veins nearly killed me. There was no way I was going to a rally with nearly every damn member. "No way."

"That wasn't a request." There was a sharpness in his eyes, an unmistakable reminder of what this man was capable of. Government sanctioned or not, Mason Stone was a killer.

I looked up at him like I was just slapped. *How dare he?*

"I tried to spare you from all this, Elisha, but now you're here. With what you know about me, I can't let you out of my sight till tomorrow night. I have too much riding on your silence."

"Why not try to kill me, then?" I shot up from the stairs with fire in my eyes. "No one knows I'm here. I have nowhere to go. Even if you force me to come with you, you can't watch me all the time."

The color in my knuckles drained from how tightly I clenched my fists. I didn't fully know why I was goading him, but I just couldn't help it. I was cornered and lashing out. I needed to vent some of the fear and anger that had consumed me.

"I'm a loose end in your grand plan. What's stopping you from killing me in my sleep tonight?" I walked toward him defiantly.

When I had taken him, it was because he was a wanted man. How could I have possibly known about any of this? The whole world was against me, and all I could do was flail and yell. If I couldn't blame Mason, then who *could* I blame?

"What's stopping you from killing me right now?" I shoved him, but the mountain of muscle and scars barely budged. Venom dripped from my gaze.

A lesser man would've slapped or shoved me back, but not Mason. He must have seen it for what it was. His sharp, defined edges seemed to soften slightly.

"Trust." There was no hostility in his voice when he responded.

That's all it took to see how wrong I was.

"Trust," I repeated distantly. "Real trust? No bullshit?"

"That's all I'm asking," he quietly replied.

"Okay," I said, taking a deep breath. I thought back to the file I had on Mason's chapter of the Broken Veins. Who knew how accurate that was. If I was going with him to Memphis, I needed to know what to expect. "But I want everything. Tell me everything about your club, and everything about the deal you have with the FBI. I need to know what we're walking into. I don't want to be in the dark anymore. Lay all your cards on the table."

"Everything?" He raised his eyebrows and crossed his arms.

"Everything," I insisted, sitting down on a nearby stool.

"Ah, hell." Mason groaned, planting his hands on his hips in resignation. "Okay. Let me tell you about a guy named Swift."

# Chapter 7
## MASON



"What's this all about?"

"You tell us, Swift," Double D casually replied, as if he had all the time in the world.

"Are you fucking with me, Double D?"

Double D lit a cigarette, casting half his mustached face in a wash of hard orange. It was pitch black otherwise; even the moon was afraid to come out tonight. The only other light in the dense enclosure of trees came from the headlights of our bikes, which were all aimed at Swift, our vice president.

Double D, our MC pres, looked past Swift, past the inky trees, and into memory. He rubbed his brow. "I've been to this park no less than five times, always to a different spot. Roughly to the same area, though. More or less. I took my kids to the beach here once for swimming. One of the little bastards got bit by a dog."

Double D chuckled to himself, then sighed. "The other four times were always with the club. Kinda like this, except this time is special, Swift. This is the first time I came here as a Broken Veins pres."

"So what's the occasion, Pres? This some sort of celebration?" Swift brushed his hair back and cracked a nervous smile. It was midspring, and the air still had a nip of chill to it. The row of headlights behind us picked up the glossy shine of sweat on his forehead.

"In a way." Pres walked down the line that separated the five of us from Swift. We'd parked the bikes in a similar row on the path behind us. Double D slipped in and out of shadows as he passed by each of us. He looked like he was walking through the world's slowest strobe. He finally stopped in from of me and clapped a hand on my shoulder. "This is your first time to Wharton State Park, isn't it, Mason?"

"Yeah," I replied with indifference. Thanks to being backlit by the bikes, my face was cast in shadow. Double D couldn't see that I was sweating too. At least I hoped he couldn't. "I'm not much of a nature guy. It's nice enough." I shrugged. "Serene."

"Yes!" Pres exclaimed. He slapped my chest with exuberance. Double D had an offbeat and explosive temperament that was abrupt and terrifying. It was how he kept everyone in line. "Serene. I like that. Good word. It is serene. You know why that is?"

I shrugged again. I'd been in the club long enough to know that it was best to just let him go. He'd get to his point sooner or later. That way I didn't run the risk of interrupting him. Double D hated interruptions.

"Breathe it in. Over a hundred acres of protected, undeveloped land. All a stone's throw from downtown Philly. Here, you could walk for hours and not see another living soul. It's the perfect place for all sorts of things. Camping. Cookouts. A little"—Pres started rocking his hips—"afternoon delight with a slice of sweetness on the side. This guy knows what the fuck I'm talking about." He laughed, shaking my shoulder.

Then, like the flip of a switch, he was all business again.

The pres turned back to Swift, who shuffled with discomfort at the renewed gaze. In a low, dull voice, Double D said, "However, the only reason the MC ever comes here is to bury bodies."

Swift was beginning to grasp what was also dawning on me as well. There weren't going to be any party favors. One of us wasn't leaving here alive tonight.

"D…." Swift's smile grew at the same rate as his anxiety. "I thought you said this was a celebration?"

"You said that, Swift, not me. But you know what? You're right, it is a celebration. You see, gentlemen, today is the day we get to kill a rat. And that's always worth celebrating." Double D pulled his gun and leveled it at Swift.

"Whoa, whoa. I'm no fucking rat. I'm the VP, for fuck's sake!" Swift protested, throwing his hands in the air and backing away a step.

"D, is this fer real?" Skip asked. He was a product of his time in the seventies. He was also the club's oldest active member.

"'Fraid so, Skip. A little birdy told me you sponsored

a rat." Double D cocked his big revolver. He liked revolvers because they could cock without launching a bullet from the chamber. They were dramatic. Great for interrogations. Pres also played with it when bored or when he wanted to fuck with people.

"Naw, man, I did the due diligence. Swifty was clean as a whistle," Skip argued.

"I saw the pictures of our man here all buddy-buddy with the feds. So either he's always been a rat, or he's just trying it out. Don't matter. Rules are rules."

"'Sides, anyone ever seen Swift kill anyone?" Ginge added. He was our sergeant-at-arms. He was also the biggest, angriest Scottish bastard I'd ever known.

The other guys mulled it over, then decided they hadn't.

Double D resumed. "We all know informants can't commit murder or else they'll—"

Swift cried out. "Don't do this, D. You're making a mistake! I'm not a fucking—"

The pres shot Swift in the knee for interrupting. Swift stood for a moment, growling back a scream. Soon the strain of the weight became too much for him and he collapsed.

"As I was saying." Double D cocked his head in a tic that indicated his growing irritation. He really hated interruptions. "You know." He turned his attention to me. "Now that I think about it, I've never seen Mason kill anybody either."

Everyone turned to look at me. The brisk night did little to cool the nervous heat I was giving off. It felt like there was a goddamn spotlight on me. It was always kill or be killed; I knew that when I had first joined up with the Broken Veins. Up until now, I'd always found a way around both. Was my luck running out?

Pres handed me his gun and stepped to the side. With a little reluctance, I took it. I didn't have a choice. No one turned down the pres.

"Yeah, let's see it, new blood." Spaz shoved me forward.

*New blood.* Two goddamn years and they still thought of me as the new guy. I wondered if I'd ever be on equal footing with these assholes. I couldn't murder Swift, though not because I was fond of the guy. I wasn't. I didn't dislike him either. He was just as bad as the rest of them. I could justify most of the morally ambiguous things I did, given the situation. But not cold-blooded murder.

That was about as black and white as it gets.

"Fucking do him already!" Spaz had short-cropped hair and kept himself clean-shaven. He did it to hide the fact that the facial hair he could grow was patchy and made him look like a teenager. He was younger than I was, but not by much. He was also brash, impatient, and usually too fucked-up to keep his mouth shut. "Unless you're a cop too, Mason. Are you? Are you a cop, you fucking faggot?"

We didn't get along.

"Watch your mouth, Spaz." I turned the gun on him instead. "Or the second body that drops tonight will be the one that hasn't hit puberty yet."

I was stalling, looking for an angle. Maybe if I riled up Spaz enough, I could get out of this somehow. I didn't care if they murdered Swift or not. I just knew it couldn't be me who pulled the trigger.

"Fuck you, man!" Spaz responded as I thought he would, by pulling his own gun.

"Enough!" Pres put a hand on my shoulder again, this time to break up the fight. "Jesus, you're like a fucking married couple. Spaz, put the gun away. Mason, turn around an—"

That's when the first shot went off. It grazed my shoulder and caught everyone by surprise. For a moment there, before he dove away like a startled pigeon, I thought it was Spaz who shot me. It wasn't him; the direction was all wrong. It came from the other side of me.

It was Swift. It dawned on me that we'd never taken his gun.

The second shot sent the other guys scattering, but not me. Not because I was trying to be tough, there was just no cover anywhere near me. There was no place to run.

Swift was fucked and he knew it. Shooting his way out would be the only chance he had. He had his sights set on Double D, but anyone would do. I just happened to be the easiest target.

I turned and ducked. We both fired simultaneously. He missed. I didn't. My bullet caught the prone man in the head, killing him instantly.

"Fuck! Anyone hit?" Skip asked, peering out from behind a tree.

"Yeah, but I'm good." I checked my shoulder while watching the blood drain out of the back of Swift's head. Taking a life never sat well with me. I avoided violence when I could, but when I couldn't and I had to step up… I did what I had to.

I've found that when pressed by the threat of death, some men hesitated. The difference between me and them was lying in the dirt over there. When there was no time to think, you had to act or someone else would act for you.

"Hot damn, that was some fine shooting, Mason." Pres walked back over and threw an arm around me, patting my side. "Fucking A! You get a gold star for the day!"

I swallowed my distaste of the celebration, but I played my part all the same. "Can I spend that star on a beer?" I asked, applying pressure to the stinging wound.

"That's the only goddamn thing it's good for! Mason the fucking cowboy. Shit, I think we just found your fucking nickname, brother!" Double D mimicked a quick draw at high noon. "Cowboy. Fuck yeah."

"You can get up now, Spaz." I kicked his legs. Spaz had thrown himself to the ground behind me, hoping to use me as a shield. *His courage abounds.* "Do we need to change your diaper?"

"It wasn't that fucking impressive," Spaz muttered. "Fucking lucky is all. I could've made that shot ten times over. I'm not impressed." He got up, dusting himself off, and walked over to the corpse. "Shoot at us, huh?" He pulled his dick out and started pissing in wide arcs over Swift's body. Then he focused his stream on the ex-Broken Vein's face. "You like that, you little bitch? Fucking faggot fuck."

"Congratulations, Spaz. You just claimed the honor of giving our snitch a proper burial," Double D announced.

"Wait, what?" Spaz whipped his head toward the rest of us.

"Dude, you fucking pissed on it, man. That's all you, brother," Skip replied, shaking his head.

"Mason is the new blood. He has to do it," Spaz replied with indignation. He shook his cock to get the last few drops out, then put it back in his pants.

"The cowboy is wounded. He can't shovel, man." Skip unfastened the spade from his bike and tossed it to Spaz, who caught it high on the handle. He had to shimmy to the side to keep the wooden pole from swinging down and nut-checking him.

"Seriously, guys?" Spaz looked at me like I would somehow help him out. I smiled and shrugged. It was out of my hands. "Oh, that's some fucking bullshit!"

"Get to it, Spaz. Don't make me have Cowboy shoot you in the face too." Pres laughed and everyone else joined in too.

Spaz turned his back on them, grumbling. "Fine, whatever. I don't give a fuck." Then he started to dig.

I headed back to my bike to dress my shoulder when Double D stopped me. "It strikes me that, amidst all the excitement, I almost forgot. Ratchet wants a sit-down with you."

"Ratchet? What the fuck for?"

"I guess you'll find out when we get to Arkansas." Pres smiled at me. It was the grin of a hungry lion running alongside a gazelle or a zebra. Then he slapped me on the back. "Welcome to the big leagues, Cowboy."

# Chapter 8
## MASON



"Federal agents are not allowed to shoot people in the head, Mr. Stone. I thought that went without saying when we told you not to commit any crimes."

I knew I was going to get reamed for what happened. I just expected I'd be able to at least get in the car first. The stranger behind the driver seat was wearing a dark suit and held up an FBI-issued badge.

"You heard the tape. I didn't have any choice. Where's Clark?" I closed the door of the agent's nondescript family sedan behind me.

"I heard you executed a guy." The man in the suit coldly looked back at me. He leaned against the driver side window and massaged his graying temple.

"*After* I was shot." I rolled up my sleeve to show him. The bandage still had red stains from bleeding through. "It was self-defense. Now, where the hell is Agent Clark?"

"That's dubious at best, *Cowboy*. Clark was reassigned. I'm Mr. Harris. I'm your handler from now on. The FBI's new director has been doing a lot of reassigning lately, so now you're my fucking headache."

"I barely have time to learn your names before they switch you people out."

"Don't go adding me to your Christmas card list. I won't be in this shit assignment long either." The new guy shrugged. These disconnected government assholes only saw me as an expendable chess piece.

"Where are we at with WITSEC?" I shook my head, finding my composure. "How much more evidence do you need from me?"

"After the stunt you pulled last night?" Harris scoffed.

"For fuck's sake. Feels like I'm talking to a wall. Nothing was pulled. He shot at me. I put him down. I've been doing this for two years now. How. Much. Longer?" I balled my fists. Dealing with these pricks was so damn frustrating.

"Until we say otherwise, Mr. Stone." He narrowed his eyes at me and waited until I calmed down to continue. "You have a meeting with Jacob 'Ratchet' Williams, known arms dealer and distributor. Get his plans on tape and implicate his contacts."

"If you're looking to bring down that Broken Veins chapter, it won't work. He's not an officer. Ratchet is just another member, like me."

"We're after much bigger fish than your bicycle gang. We don't want to topple the Broken Veins. We want to take down the gun trade that they're running transportation for. The Broken Veins have no national structure, so it's always been difficult to use RICO against them. The Racketeer

Influenced and Corrupt Organizations act that helps us deal with organized crime—"

"I know what RICO is," I interrupted. Honestly, I couldn't give a fuck about the bigger picture here. Let the gods and monsters have at it—I just wanted out. "What do I get out of this?"

"Are you becoming bored with the deal you cut? You just say the word. We'll release the hold we have on your file, and you'll be back in North Carolina in no time. We're keeping a cell warm for you just in case. I'm sure the men you helped put behind bars since becoming an informant would love to see you in gen pop."

I kept quiet. We both knew they had me by the balls. If I went back to prison, I'd be choking on my own blood within a week.

"Not so entitled now, are you, Mr. Stone?"

At another time in my life, I'd have slammed his face into the steering wheel without hesitation. I'd like to think I'd changed, that that version of me was long gone. After all, I fought the law, and the law won.

But I could feel it bubbling right under the surface. That prideful rage. It never truly went away; I just had better control now. My main focus now was to survive, and to do that, I needed to stay out of prison.

"I didn't ask for this assignment. Personally, criminal scum like you… I hope you get what's coming to you." Harris slowed his speech down to a patronizing crawl. "I'll use small sentences so you can understand me. You get *me* Ratchet. I get *you* an interview with Witness Security Protection."

"Interview? What the fuck? That was supposed to be a done deal!" I quickly caught myself and settled down. "The deal—"

"Is whatever the fuck we say it is," he sharply continued. "WITSEC is a gateway to a new life, Mr. Stone. It's a fresh start. A whole new beginning. And it's extremely expensive to the taxpayer, so of course they have to interview you. They need to make sure that, after they've spent all this money on you, you're trustworthy enough to keep the secret."

"Trustworthy?" I laughed at the absurdity of it. "My whole life is a secret. If I told anyone who I really was, I wouldn't need WITSEC. I'd need a fucking coroner." If any of my old contacts found out where I was or who I was now, pieces of me would turn up across three states.

"Same difference to me." Harris shrugged indifferently.

"Are we done?" I sighed, feeling exhausted and utterly defeated. I just wanted this to be over.

Harris fished a stick recorder out of his breast pocket and slapped it into my chest. He looked at me, holding it there.

"If *anything* goes wrong with this meeting, I will crush you under the full weight of federal law." He released the stick and moved his hand away. "*Now* we're done. Get the fuck out of my car."

# Chapter 9
## MASON

The ride to Memphis was exactly what I needed, especially after laying everything bare with Elisha. It was both terrifying and freeing to tell her everything. She could completely destroy me if she wanted to. Now all I could do was trust that she wouldn't.

Trust.

What a novel notion. I hadn't trusted someone in as long as I could remember.

I hoped I made the right call with her. I desperately wanted to believe I did, but I'd been burned *so* many times before....

I swallowed hard at the thought and just prayed this time would be different.

At least riding was always something that gave me solace.

The road was like a switch that I could only hit at about eighty miles an hour. When the howl of the engine melted into the roar of the wind and became one booming sound, my brain shifted from thought to *feel*.

There was still a dull fire in my wrist from the cuffs, and a lingering exhaustion in my muscles. I twisted the throttle. The pain dimmed with the slow climb of RPMs. It was a relief that came only with adrenaline and a careless disregard of fear.

I felt it in my bones. The steady thrum of the pavement under my wheels screamed, *Faster! You can outrun it all!*

The highway went on forever. Sometimes it was completely empty, a barren strip of blacktop that waved in the midday heat like a black river. Other times there was a sparse smattering of cars. They drove slow enough that passing them seemed like an obstacle course.

The open road was a kind of crowded loneliness that did weird things to people. In a car, long drives used to hypnotize me and put me to sleep. I had to blast music and pound energy drinks to get through the monotony of the passing hours.

On a bike, though…. Fuck, I was a goddamn king!

Riding flushed out all the distractions in my life. It was pure. Simple. And unlike the rest of the heaping piles of shit I dealt with, it all made sense. On a bike was the only place I was truly in control. I decided if I lived or died, not the feds, not the Broken Veins. Me.

Everything else fell away, except that intoxicating power of freedom.

All the covert evidence-gathering crap that kept me out of jail had no end in sight. It had been two long, hard, excruciating years buddying up with murderers and psychopaths. But what was that in the face of a twenty-year sentence?

Up until recently, I had no idea how long they'd keep me as a confidential informant, a *rat*. I lived day to day with no thought of tomorrow. How could I?

I was one lie, one mistake, one casual slipup away from being found out by my club and executed. The feds could also drop me at any time if I didn't record enough info to be useful to my handler.

Then I'd be sent back to prison, surrounded by the guys I turned on to get the deal in the first place. With my cover blown, it'd only be a matter of time until I caught a shiv between my ribs.

Yeah, I ate steak, slept in my own bed, and fucked whoever I wanted, but so what? The flavor of life was drained out of all of it. I was once a snake. Now I was just the empty husk of its molted skin, waiting to be stepped on.

I was in a prison of a whole different kind.

On the road, I felt like I'd escaped that, even if only for a little while.

Then I met Elisha.

I'd had other girls on my bike, of course, but most of them were just to keep up appearances. I never stuck my dick in crazy. The MC's hangarounds were usually burnt-out whores who were hooked on our drugs or the outlaw lifestyle.

The Broken Veins chewed those girls up.

With Elisha, it was so different.

I took a moment to focus on her arms wrapped around me. It wasn't a thought or a feeling but a sensation, almost like a fond memory that I hadn't lived yet.

I'd always felt so fucked before I met her.

In the quiet, low times when the crushing weight became unbearable, I always asked myself, *Then what?* If, by some miracle, I survived long enough to satisfy the feds and they let me go, then what?

Where would I go? What would I do?

They didn't give a shit about any of that. They'd get their convictions, their pats on the back, and then move on to some *other* asshole fuckup.

I had some family left, but they'd written me off a long time ago. I couldn't blame them. There was a reason I was sent to prison in the first place. I couldn't reach out to any of them. That time had come and gone.

The time I spent with Elisha, fighting for her… it was the best I'd ever felt.

I was still driven by my obligations, of course. But by keeping her alive—hell, by just being near her—I felt a contentedness I didn't think was possible.

Yes, even with clothes on it was easy to see she had a body to raise an army and go to war for, but it wasn't just physical attraction that kept her in my every waking thought. It was the fact that Elisha was a good person. Coming from a criminal background, *goodness* was rarer than a diamond-encrusted unicorn.

How could I let the Broken Veins, who ground up goodness with abandon, get their sadistic hands on her?

When she was with me, my world wasn't complete shit. If survival was a *how*, then she was quickly becoming my *why*.

I knew it was a fairy tale. There were a million reasons we'd never end up together, but for the moment, as selfish as it was, I allowed myself to dream. She gave me a sense of purpose, and for the first time in as long as I could remember, I didn't need to ask myself, *Why bother?*

The silhouette of Memphis had just started darkening as we approached it. The sun reflected brilliantly off an out-of-place pyramid and the river behind the city. It gave the whole place an otherworldly glow.

It was still early when we checked into the hotel. I hadn't realized how quickly we'd made the journey.

"Ever been to Memphis before?" I asked Elisha once we got settled into our room.

"Once when I was very little, but I was too young to remember any of it clearly," Elisha replied almost automatically. She had a dull, disinterested tone. I chalked it up to road fatigue initially. We did just spend half a day on a missile with wheels, after all.

The closer we got to Arkansas, the realer everything became. I couldn't hide behind my handlebars forever. I also couldn't do anything to speed it up or delay the inevitable. What I needed was a break from thinking about the things I couldn't change.

It was only then that I realized the ride had the opposite effect on her. Where I found it to be my only form of freedom, it trapped her in her own head. Where I left my demons behind to chase me, Elisha's demons firmly affixed themselves in her mind and drowned out everything else.

I watched her unpack and sort her clothes with a

disconnected weariness about her. She was just going through the motions in a haze. Knowing for certain the bounty she'd been so driven to collect was false clearly weighed heavily on her.

That fiery spirit within her seemed tarnished, on the verge of being altogether extinguished. It was hard to look at.

Maybe she needed a break from all of this as well. I glanced over to a welcome brochure on the bed's pillow. 'Welcome to Memphis, home of the blues,' it said. What better place to lose ourselves than here?

"What do you do for fun, Elisha? When you're not throwing down with angry bikers?"

"Fun?" she asked, the lights in her mind started kicking back on.

"Yeah. It's a foreign concept, but you might have heard of it."

She narrowed her eyes at my verbal prodding, then slipped into a thoughtful state.

"I like to dance," she blurted. The fact that it took her that long to answer convinced me that she might need a distraction even more than me.

How long had it been since she'd had any actual fun?

"Let's see what we can find." I nodded toward the door.

"You're letting me leave the room?" She searched my face carefully.

"I can bust out the cuffs if you really want, but unless it's foreplay, I don't think you'll like it."

Her face reddened. Elisha embodied professionalism,

but the sexual tension between us when I was cuffed to that pipe and she was undressing me was undeniable.

"You're not worried that I might make a run for it and ruin the meeting for you tomorrow?"

"I'm giving this whole trust thing a try." My tone was nonchalant. "Why, should I be?"

Elisha's eyes flashed wide. She was startled by the straightforwardness of the question. She had every reason to try to run.

"No," she said as much to herself as to me. "I promised you I wouldn't."

"All right, then."

She scoffed at my cavalier attitude about the whole thing. We both knew she couldn't shoot me, and even if she did sneak away at some point, she wouldn't blow my cover. The skeptic in me believed that much, at least.

More than anything I wanted to keep her close so I could protect her. My club was still out there, and they would still be keeping an eye out for her regardless of what I said about the incident. That wasn't the only reason I wanted to keep her with me, but it was the least selfish one.

I had a feeling that one way or another, tomorrow night would be the last time I saw Elisha. That notion emptied me out inside. I had to make the most of every second we spent together.

Again, I motioned toward the door.

"Yeah, why not?" She finally shrugged, and with a guarded smile, she walked toward the door.

I stopped her. "There is one condition."

*Here it comes*, said her expression.

"You put on something that's not a three-piece suit."

Her eyes flashed in surprise.

"You're the one that's underdressed," she shot back, but I wouldn't budge on it. "Fine," she stated with exasperation. "I'll leave the blazer."

She rolled it off her shoulders, revealing a cream-colored silk button-up top. I could clearly see the straps and lines of her bra beneath the fabric. It was a shame to see her stop at just the blazer. I hadn't been able to make it a few hours without fantasizing what it would be like seeing the rest of her clothes hitting the bed as well.

"So," I said, clearing my mind as much as possible. I didn't want to hit the town with my cock at half-mast. I held our room's door open for her. "You going to be my tour guide?"

"I think a few things might have changed since I was roaming the mean streets of Memphis in my baby carrier." It was good to see a little humor return to her.

You wouldn't know it from how quiet and casual the hotel was on our way out, but the streets were packed with people. There was some sort of music festival in the area. Blues, jazz, and rock spilled out of every open door and window. The gathering masses strolled by respectfully, their baser instincts held in check by the starkness of the dwindling daylight.

*When nightfall hits, this place is going to turn into bedlam.*

After a considerable wait, we got dinner at a small but

full-to-the-gills BBQ joint called BB Deville's. It was hands down the best pulled pork I'd ever had. Soon enough we found ourselves back outside taking in the sights.

The neon signs made the slit of sky between the closely packed buildings on Beale Street look like a swirling glass of full-bodied wine. People had arrived in droves. We weren't walking anywhere in particular, just away from the occasional deafening music coming from certain places.

Between the noise and the rush of bodies, Elisha clung to me to avoid being separated by the human tide. I didn't mind, wrapping an arm around her lower back and making space for us. No one batted an eye at us being together. People were far more progressive here than in my shitty hometown.

I abruptly jerked her against my chest to pull her from the path of an oncoming horse-drawn carriage. Her small figure pressed tightly to me, she put her ear to my chest and watched the horse slowly trot by.

Elisha wrapped her arm around me, and I could feel her heartbeat through my stomach. I lowered my nose to the top of her head and took in her scent. In some ways, having her that close was more intimate than sex could ever hope to be. She gave me warmth, and I gave her protection.

It felt normal, natural, almost like we were an actual couple. It wasn't something I even knew I wanted, and now that I did, I wasn't sure I could ever let it go.

She and I… was this what it would be like?

I was unfocused, lost in a fantasy, when she pulled at my arm. She spotted the bikes before I did.

At first glance, I didn't know who they belonged to. The tightly packed row of motorcycles was far enough away that I couldn't make out any insignia. I'd left my vest in the hotel room just in case something like this happened, but if those bikes belonged to the Broken Veins, they'd recognize me regardless of what I was wearing.

Elisha was quicker on the draw than I was, pulling me into the nearest open door.

"Hey, y'all." We were greeted right away by the soothing, unhurried voice of a well-dressed older man. He sat on a chair in front of the register with an inviting smile. He was only a few shades lighter than his rich brown three-piece suit and tie. "You havin' fun out there?"

"Hi," Elisha replied to the voice before turning to find the man.

"You can call me Sam. Anything I can help you with?" he asked with modesty and patience.

"Oh, no, thanks, we're just browsing." Elisha looked around, realizing it was a music shop she'd pulled us into. "Actually, yes." She turned back to me, her eyes filled with mischief. I knew what she was up to, but before I could say anything, she asked, "Do you have any violins?"

*Oh hell....*

"Yes, ma'am." Sam used the counter to help lift his old frame up and then walked to the back corner of the shop.

"Elisha, this really isn't—" I eyed her, spreading my hands. I was thinking about the men outside and who they were. Did this place have a back door? Could we duck out unseen?

"You know of a better way to blend in?" She dismissed my impatience with a matter-of-fact shrug.

I thought on that a moment and really couldn't. No MC biker would set foot in a place like this unless they were told to do so.

She grabbed my shirt and pulled me with her past a wall of guitars.

"Besides, you mentioned something about 'Amazing Grace.'" She smirked.

The old man showed me his stock of violins and bows, each freshly rosined and on display in their own case. I grabbed one by its polished rosewood neck and placed the round bottom on my shoulder like I'd done countless times before. But that was another life....

I couldn't suppress my half grin as my rusty, sluggish fingers contorted over the chords. Mrs. K, my music teacher, would've ribbed me for my lack of grace. I was irrationally glad that she wasn't in the store.

I thought on the song, humming it softly to myself. It'd been a long time since I'd even heard it played, let alone played it myself. The first few drags of the bow were slow, short, and too close. They cracked with the occasional honk of a mis-stroke. "I told you I was a bit rusty."

Elisha said nothing, just smiled and watched.

I cleared my throat, adjusted my grips, and started over. Again, I started slow. With the first few strokes, I worked out the tinny sound from my stumbling, rigid fingers. It was when I closed my eyes and concentrated that I began to hear the song as it was supposed to be played.

It was like falling off a bicycle; once you learned, you never really forgot how.

As I relaxed and my confidence grew, the song went from recited half-memory to practiced art. I was never a natural at the tricky instrument, but I did enjoy playing it. The sound always calmed me down.

It felt good to just create something pleasant.

I'd reached the end of the song before I knew it and opened my eyes. Elisha looking back at me was what I saw first. She was clearly impressed and had the faint glow of a smitten fan. She lightly clapped and mouthed, "Wow."

"Not too shabby, son." Sam nodded with the cool reserve of an actual musician. "Careful, hon," he addressed Elisha. "He's bound to break a few hearts, you let him keep practicing."

Looking past him, I saw two bikers walk by. One stopped, cupping his eyes and pushing his face into the glass to get a good look inside. He was looking right at me. I froze, switching to a tight overhand grip on the violin like it was a baseball bat just in case they came in and I needed it as a weapon. The biker's vest slapped against the window when he leaned forward, and his patch was clearly visible.

They were Warlocks MC and were probably here for the festival. I breathed a little easier. They weren't a rival or an ally. They were just another club. Totally neutral. They wouldn't know me. Without my vest, I was no different than any other scruffy asshole kicking around.

I breathed a sigh of relief. We were all right.

"She's got nothing to worry about," I said, gently

replacing the violin in its case and putting a hand on the man's shoulder. "I'll leave the heartbreaking to the professionals like you."

The old man laughed with hearty abandon.

We thanked him and stepped back out onto the street. Elisha was hesitant at first, but I explained the situation. This was apparently Warlock country. As long as we kept a healthy distance from them, they wouldn't seek us out.

"How long have you been riding for?" Elisha asked after several minutes of aimless walking. It was still too early to call it a night, so we decided to enjoy the festival.

"I'd never ridden before joining up with the Broken Veins." I could tell she had trouble believing me. "In fact," I continued, "my first full year as a prospect was spent in a beat-down pickup truck."

"What?" She laughed, a smile born of disbelief spread across her face.

"Yeah, it was perfect for hauling around members too drunk or fucked-up to drive. It was the club that gave me my first bike."

"Wait a minute." Her smile faded a bit. "So the FBI had you join a motorcycle club and didn't give you a motorcycle?"

"Our government at work." I chuckled, remembering the original conversation. "I said the same thing to them when I started. The only things I ever got from the feds were audio recorders. Informants like me were found out constantly. It was staggering. Something like 80 percent of the time, informants were caught and killed. So I guess why waste the resources on a bike? I was—I *am* completely expendable, as Harris loves to remind me."

"That's atrocious." Elisha's lips tightened and her eyebrows scrunched. "It couldn't be that often."

"Most of the time, it's not the cops that go undercover in these clubs. It's too dangerous." I nodded. "That's why they were so quick to cut me a deal when I was busted. MCs like the Broken Veins excel at flushing out rats. That's why it takes so much time to get vetted and brought in as a full patch member."

"Jesus...."

"Kind of ironic, actually. That's why the Broken Veins originally formed from the Steel Veins."

"Yeah, I've heard of them." Elisha looked off into the distance, probably recalling old case files. "They had a terrible reputation until the new guy took over, right?"

"That was before my time, but yeah. Apparently this dude named Remy led a coup against the old guard leaders and kicked out all the new, untested members of the Steel Veins so they could start vetting members properly. The club was pretty corrupt by then, so that went over like a lead balloon. All the pissed-off members that got the axe and those who didn't want anything to do with the Steel Veins going legit formed the Broken Veins. Now they vet the shit out of their members so no cops or rats get into the clubs."

"Huh," Elisha mused. "Yet here you are like a damn informant ninja."

"When the feds have you by the balls, you gotta be on your toes."

There was some silence between us for a while as we walked down the crowded street. I knew what she wanted to ask me. I wondered how long it would take for her to come out with it.

She was hesitant. Not because she was afraid to approach the subject; I figured it was because she didn't want to destroy whatever image she had of me in her head. What if I was a real scumbag, or a fucking monster like a kid killer, a cannibal, or someone who broke into nursing homes and fucked little old ladies?

"Go ahead." I broke the tension. "You can ask me."

"What did you do?" she immediately replied. "Most of your records were either redacted or missing."

"I was a thief."

She was taken aback, her demeanor lightening. *That's it?* her form seemed to say as relief washed over her. She was too lawful to ever condone stealing, but I was sure it was much better than whatever other horrible things she'd imagined I did.

"What'd you steal?"

"Expensive cars at first. We'd chop them up and sell the pieces. That's where I learned how to make real money. Logistics. I had the connections and know-how to develop the whole infrastructure. By the time I was busted, I had been pulling in thousands of dollars a day in transportation and service cuts. All the carjackers in three states came to me. By the end, I was a fucking king of underground commerce."

"That's why the bounty was so high...." It all began to

click for Elisha.

"A king's ransom." I spread my arms out and bowed slightly.

Elisha smirked and shook her head at the bad joke.

"And now you're one of the good guys?"

"Whatever keeps me out of jail." I shrugged with resignation.

Elisha furrowed her eyebrows at that, obviously disappointed by my answer. Everything I'd gleaned from her painted her as a woman with uncompromising convictions and ideals.

I could only imagine what she saw when she looked at a criminal like me.

"This costume you see isn't who I really am." I pointed to myself, not so much for the clothing I was currently wearing, but more for the lifestyle I'd had to adopt. "It's not who I wanted to be, at least. Growing up, I didn't have a lot of options. I could've just as easily slung drugs instead of stealing cars. One thing led to another, and before I knew it, I was swept up in this hurricane of undercover bullshit."

I chuckled. It sounded like I was making excuses, and maybe I was. After all, to everyone else, I was just a devil in a stolen robe and halo.

"You may not believe me. Hell, I don't know if I even believe me, but I never wanted to hurt anyone. I was just looking to survive is all."

"Bending with the direction of the wind just to survive as someone you don't like means killing the good person you could be." Elisha looked at me thoughtfully.

"You'd make one hell of a fortune cookie writer." I smiled weakly, trying to deflect the painful truths in her words. She flashed me an impatient smirk. "I'm doing the right thing now. Isn't that all that matters?"

"I don't know." She shrugged. There was an earnest honesty in her voice. "What I do know is it can be incredibly rewarding to do the right things for the *right* reasons."

Had anyone else said that to me, it would've been in a patronizing tone, and I would've brushed it off without a second thought, but not Elisha. She looked at me with concern. She was actually worried about me.

Having someone concerned about my well-being was a strange, alien sensation that made me uncomfortable. But I'd be lying if I said it wasn't nice to hear.

"What would you have done with the money?" I asked her, changing the subject. I'd worn so many masks for so long that I needed to get out of the spotlight. "If it was real?"

Elisha sighed, that sadness creeping back into her. She didn't strike me as the kind of girl who failed at the things she set her mind to. When it did happen, I bet she was extra hard on herself because of that.

"Honestly, I don't know anymore. I think I was more obsessed with getting it than I was with having it. I just needed a distraction. Everything had begun to unravel and I saw you—" She elbowed my arm playfully. "—or your bounty, rather, as a way to *fix* everything. If I just had enough money…. "

Elisha frowned at the smug expression that crept across my face. I knew she thought I was making fun of her, but that wasn't it at all. I had just been in her shoes, and I knew all too well what that obsession was like.

"That's the trick of it," I said, letting the knowing grin fade. I stopped on the sidewalk like a boulder in a rushing river of people. "Money doesn't fix problems. Not the real problems. Not the ones that matter."

Elisha was bumped into me from behind by an apologizing tourist who was trying to get by. I caught her with ease and matched her gaze. My skin crackled everywhere she touched me. In the way she looked up at me, I could see she felt it too.

Her eyes told me I was the only person on that busy street.

"You don't get it." A renewed cheer from a street performance forced her to lean in and yell in my ear just to be heard. "Without enough money for a lawyer, I can't fight Kenneth if things get really bad. Right now I am completely at his mercy."

"What are you fighting for?" I asked with genuine curiosity, the roar from the crowd dying down in the background. She looked at me like I had three heads. "It's all just stuff. Does it even make you happy?"

She went for what was probably some canned reply, but the words failed her. The question might've struck her harder than I meant it. Elisha looked troubled and struggled to answer. I couldn't fully know the distress that clouded her mind and heart. All I saw was distant pain in her upturned, yet still stunning, rich brown eyes.

It was a simple question, but sometimes they held the

hardest truths.

She frowned and looked away. I wasn't going to press her for it. The only person she owed an explanation to was herself.

It was too loud and crowded on the street. Knowing we'd both benefit from a little breathing room, I began to move us from the throng of people when some big bastard in a wide-brimmed ten-gallon hat shoved past us hard.

On instinct, I snapped a hand out and grabbed his shirt, jerking the rude prick back a step toward me. "Watch your fucking step. Apologize to the lady."

"Mason…." Elisha grabbed my arm, shaking her head. Her body language told me it wasn't worth it.

I exhaled and let him go. She was right. I was the one to stop us in human traffic. We were bound to get bumped. It had been a really good night; why ruin that by getting blood all over our clothes?

"That's right," the pasty-skinned tough guy snapped back at me. He was all piss and vinegar now that I'd let him go. It was clear that he thought the world owed him something. "Pussy whipped by a bitch."

"Excuse me?" I immediately regretted my decision to turn the other cheek.

Mr. Ten-Gallon Hat winked at her and blew her a kiss in response. My knuckles popped as my hands balled into fists. My skin was thick enough for insults aimed at me, but slights against Elisha?

That, I wouldn't tolerate.

Elisha beat me to it. My eyes shot wide as I watched her

knee him in the balls. He bent forward, his face immediately contorting in pain and shock. Then Elisha smashed him in the nose for good measure, putting the grown man on his ass in front of everyone. Passersby slowed down for the spectacle, but only for a moment before continuing on. Those who'd heard the exchange smiled and nodded to Elisha. Some even congratulated her for standing up to him.

I smiled, lifting the hat from the defeated man's head.

Elisha beamed at the crowd approval but quickly began to deflate and shrink into herself slightly. Was she embarrassed at all the attention?

She grabbed my hand, pulling me off the sidewalk and through the door of an empty shop that had closed for the night. She flashed her eyebrows at me and shrugged. Her rigid stance began to loosen and relax.

Maybe she stopped me earlier because she could fight her own battles. An excited thrill shot through my body at the thought. She never failed to impress me. Her coiled, tensed form was hot as hell. I could barely stand it. She didn't take shit from anyone. It was a heady turn-on.

"To the victor go the spoils." I placed the hat on her head. "It's a good look on you."

"The hat?" She eyed me skeptically. I'd never seen her in any headwear before, and my guess was she'd tell me she wasn't a hat kind of girl. I propped myself up with both arms pressed against the door on either side of her head. Like a reverse push-up, I bent my arms and erased the distance between us.

"I was talking about the fire in your eyes." My lips

hovered over hers, grazing against them as I spoke. Her lips pulled back in a sultry smile, revealing her pearly teeth that were just slightly crooked. Imperfections had their own alluring charm. "And the hat doesn't look terrible either."

My teeth clicked against hers before they were overtaken by her plush dark maroon lips. I tasted her cherry-hinted lip balm first, then ran my tongue across her opening teeth. I'd never kissed anyone like I kissed Elisha. It was soft and sweet, wrapped in spikes of passion and dipped in lust.

Call me hardened, but with everyone else, it had been just the meaningless mashing of lips. But not her. In this small act, my soul was satiated. My body, on the other hand... it revved harder than the V2 four-stroke engine on my Harley.

The minutes sped by as the intensity of our passion grew. The hat had fallen away at some point, but neither of us paid it any mind.

Our slice of semiprivate heaven was only several feet from the main thoroughfare. When I felt her fingers dig into my waist, I knew we'd need a little more privacy.

I peeled back just enough to gingerly sink my teeth into her lower lip. "Let's get out of here." My voice was a low growl over the street music, more vibration than sound.

She nodded devilishly.

"Yeah?" I asked, looking her over skeptically. After so many miles and so many half-truths between us it was hard to believe this was actually happening.

"Don't go spoiling the mood." She gave me a knowing look. "You're not my bounty anymore. Hell, you're not even really an outlaw biker now either."

"Always the professional," I said in a low, close voice, pulling her into another kiss.

Our hotel was fifteen blocks away. Neither of us had that kind of patience.

# Chapter 10
## ELISHA

We hustled through the masses. The only pockets of space on that busy street were given to backflipping performers and a parked police cruiser. Other than that, people were everywhere. They became louder and more riotous as the night went on.

Mason barely noticed; he was a snowplow carving us a path through the crowd. I quick-stepped directly behind him, trying to keep up. One of my hands was in his, and the other was held up to protect against the occasional drunken flailing limb.

We entered a mostly vacant brick-and-concrete park. The sparse overhead spotlights cast the park's one lonely tree in a haunting bright yellow hue. Its long shadow engulfed a couple who lay on the cold stone fondling each other.

In the darkest areas with the least eyes on them, drunk, horny couples were going at it. Mostly soft-core stuff, like kissing and touching. I was envious. I was attracted to Mason the moment I saw him riding down the highway, but never in a million years would I have thought anything would happen between us. The more time I spent with him, these little nagging fantasies about what he would be like crept into my head. Now that all bets were truly off, I didn't know exactly what he had planned, but I could feel myself getting wetter as my thoughts were finally free to run wild.

Mason wrapped an arm around me as we walked out the rear entrance of the park and into an even dimmer parking lot. The music and the noise of the crowd were still booming even out here.

"Where are we going?" I asked.

He stopped abruptly a few seconds later, ignoring my question. Then Mason picked me up and slammed us against the side of a gray Hummer H2. It rocked from the impact of our bodies. The stubble of his beard lit my skin on fire and turned my brain to mush as his kisses started at my cheek then roamed hungrily. The music boomed and the crowd cheered almost as if it were meant just for us.

Everything about this—him and me in each other's arms—was unbelievable. I meant that literally. Waves of incredulity washed over me, reminding me that it wasn't long ago I was bringing Mason to justice as a fugitive. That was all gone now. Mason and I were just two people whose lives were changed irrevocably by forces beyond their control. For having such radically different backgrounds, we had a lot of things in common.

I felt for him, truly.

He dragged his mouth over my collarbone and murmured something. I was so focused on the movements of his tongue and teeth that I didn't catch it.

"What'd you say?" I asked.

He stopped, locked eyes with me, and fully articulated every word. "I'm going to fuck you—"

I thrilled at his brash, definitive tone with a wide smile. This was really happening! I'd spent so much time convincing myself of all the reasons it was impossible to have sex with him, despite how much my body ached for him, and now to be able to let all that go... was exhilarating!

"—right here," he finished.

"Wait, what? Here?" My eyes shot wide. Were we really going to do this out in the open? It was dark, sure, but it wasn't pitch-black. We were still in a parking lot; if someone were looking for us, they'd find us.

This was insane.

He didn't answer. Instead, he jerked my shirt up and kissed down my stomach. Mason was relentless, and my ability to care about what was proper or even legal dulled with every pass of his lips.

His caress down my side left electric trails in my skin that crackled all the way up to the back of my head like dozens of little firecrackers detonating. My inhibitions fell away; all that mattered was the next touch.

He unclasped my pants when I heard some people walk by, but if they noticed us, they didn't seem to care. That's when I heard the click. Mason had tested the back door of the Hummer, and it swung right open.

"Whoa!" Up against a vehicle was one thing, but having sex *inside* someone's car? "That's crazy. You can't!"

"Watch me." He lifted me off the side of the truck

with ease. I might as well have been on a roller coaster of tattooed muscle; I was just along for the ride. I crashed into the leather-upholstered back seat. I still couldn't believe we were doing this period, let alone in a stranger's car. "It's their own damn fault for not locking their door."

I went to sit up, but with one heavy palm on my chest, Mason pushed me back down. *Oh really?* With Kenneth, I was always in charge when we had sex. Mason was obviously a different force entirely.

I sat up again; defiance was hardwired into my nature. Again, I was pushed back down. This time his hand stayed there, pinning me to the seat. I should never be able to trust him, but we had so much history together in such a short time.

Even still there was that part of my brain that reminded me what he was. Undercover or not, Mason was once a criminal and was still a dangerous biker. And now he was free to do with me as he pleased.

If it were anyone else I wouldn't have been able to trust them, but Mason was different inside and out. He was a book with the wrong cover—a second-chance romance dressed as a crime drama.

I didn't know if I could handle him, but I needed to find out.

Every thought in my head muddled uselessly together as he wrenched my pants and panties down to my knees. With his every kiss down my lower stomach all I could think about was what the first touch of his tongue on my clit would feel like. My pussy flared with heat and wetness in anticipation. No one had ever gone down on me before. I was both nervous and excited.

God, he was so sure and dominant. It was like my hidden desires were pages in a book he was reading. I never dreamed of telling Kenneth to touch me this way, but with Mason, I didn't even need to ask.

I creamed the second I felt his lips on my inner thigh, working their way along my slit. He plunged his face into my pussy. I thought I was prepared for his tongue, but it was his whole mouth that lay into me. It was utter bliss, a sensation I'd never felt before.

My legs twitched as he made my pussy serve him. A shock ran up my body when I felt his teeth tug at my clit. I shrieked.

He paused for a fleeting moment to make sure I was all right. I immediately covered my mouth in embarrassment, but Mason didn't mind. He switched between sucking my clit and exploring my hidden folds with his tongue.

I closed my eyes and rode the waves of lust. My muscles tightened. I came hard.

Mason didn't stop.

My eyes snapped open. I was close again, and it didn't look like he had any intention of slowing. I grabbed a tuft of his hair and pulled, but he wouldn't budge. I crashed forward into his palm, which still pinned me down. "Oh God. I'm coming again. You're killing me."

"I'll stop when you scream it."

I felt every word through my sensitive lips. I was soaked. He didn't slow, just drank me in and kept going.

The crushing waves of pleasure threatened to ruin me. "I'm coming! I'm coming!" The scream came from all the way down to my heels. My head was spinning when he pulled away. My heart was beating so hard I felt it in my fingernails.

I watched as he tore his shirt off. The soft reflected light from the park lit him just enough for his sculpted outline to glow. I didn't see his cock at first, not until he turned to fish the condom out of his pants. It was massive, somehow even bigger than I'd imagined.

I lay on the sticky, clinging leather with my legs hanging limply open. "That was incredible."

"That was nothing." He unrolled the condom down the length of his stone-hard cock. He looked me over, taking in every glistening inch of me. "Goddamn, girl," Mason growled.

His hungry tone sent a shiver through me. Mason was a giant of a man. The things he could do to me if he wanted… I was completely at his mercy. What had I unleashed?

The thought of being fully taken by him should have terrified me, but it didn't. All my nerve endings vibrated with anticipation, excitement, and yearning instead.

I wanted him to take me.

The leather beneath me squealed as Mason grabbed my hips and jerked me toward him. He slipped my pants off and hoisted my knees back to my chest like bent TV antennae.

My pussy spread open, aching for his cock. His fat head slid over my engorged clit, lighting my senses up in another frenzied wave. *Do it!* I was losing my mind. Why did he have to torture me? He knew what I wanted.

"Say it."

First he had me screaming, and now I had to beg? Maybe he was a monster after all, making me squirm to be filled up. My pussy throbbed for him. "You bastard," I weakly moaned.

Mason slapped my pussy lips with his cock and teased. Every strike sent tremors rippling through me. "Say it."

"Fine! I'll say anything you want, just fuck me!" I screamed, then immediately gasped. I rarely swore. It wasn't a habit I'd ever gotten into.

*Fuck.* I always found the word distasteful. I almost never used it; it wasn't professional. I thought I was above that. Apparently not. Between using it when I was being attacked by Gintin and now, the big bad biker was certainly rubbing off on me.

And I wanted him to do a lot more than that.

"The mouth on you. Naughty girl," he teased.

Mason squeezed my thighs to the point of pain, then pushed his long thick cock inside me. My eyes glazed over. My inner walls spread and tightened around him. With every inch I expected him to bottom out. Maybe it was the position he had me in, but I couldn't believe how deep he was.

My lungs seemed to shrink and flutter at the same time. He'd buried himself up to the stem. It was so tight, but I was so wet that I could take him. I felt him flex inside me. He withdrew and then slammed back in until a rhythm formed. My brain was wiped; all I could focus on was his cock pushing and pulling.

I remembered where we were. My adrenaline spiked every time a car door slammed or a horn honked. Were we putting on a show for people? Some of them must have seen us. If they did, no one said anything. There were no shouts of protest, at least.

I'd never realized what a thrill sex in public was.

My eyes had closed at some point, and when I reopened them, I saw Mason's tan form in vivid detail, the headlights from a leaving car bathing him clearly. The intensity in his eyes and face riddled my arms and legs with goose bumps. He didn't give a damn about our surroundings.

I was all there was to him. And that felt amazing.

He loomed before me, statuesque, sculpted muscle, and danger. He moved me with such ease and power that I felt like I was being fucked by a god.

Another set of crossing headlights coated him, and this time the burn scars that ran up his side flared in their discoloration. They were much bigger than I remembered. How horrible that must have been for him....

The thrusts stopped. I actually whimpered when he pulled out. Before I could protest, his viselike grip flipped me onto my stomach. I got excited again. From behind was one of my favorite positions.

He pushed into me again, even deeper now. My back arched as I struggled to take all of him. How could he be so damn big? He placed a hand on my hip and pushed my tits into the supple leather seats. It got me so hot that my blood began to boil.

I met his every thrust with a push back. My ass cheeks were worn raw from slapping into his hips. Minutes, hours, or days later, lights sparkled behind my eyes. I was on the cusp of coming again. My legs were quickly turning to Jell-O. I couldn't stop the muscles in my pussy from contracting in a thousand little shock waves.

How could I have resisted this for so long? He was unbelievable, better than anything I'd ever experienced.

When he pulled my hair, I lost it. My whole body locked up, and I was finished. I screamed and came so loud and hard that I thought I lost my voice and went blind. All my senses were simultaneously numb and exploding.

My pussy's sudden tensing strangled his pulsing cock. I milked his molten cum into the condom. I wished the latex barrier wasn't there; I wanted to feel his pearly seed fill me up.

Mason slid out and lay on my back. He kissed up my spine.

"Jesus," I said, out of breath. "That could only be kinkier if we used the cuffs."

"Your pussy's all the kink I need." He flashed a wicked grin, then rolled the condom off and tossed it. "Everything else just gets in the way."

"I'll keep that in mind." I moaned, turning onto my back and pulling him to me.

"For next time?" Mason's eyebrow arched up. "Only if you're good."

I smirked at what his definition of 'good' was.

"What do you say we just take the Hummer?" He smiled again. "Go for a little joyride."

My eyes flashed. *Is he serious?* Fooling around was one thing, but that was crossing a line.

Mason seemed to enjoy the look of worry on my face, but eventually he just winked at me playfully.

"Jerk." I slapped his shoulder, then pushed him off. He just laughed. He seemed to like making me squirm. I'd have to remember that.

The music had begun to die down, and there was an influx of drunken festivalgoers returning to their cars. "We should go before the owners of this car stumble back to see the mess we made."

Mason reluctantly nodded, and once we were presentable enough, we headed back to our hotel room.

"What happened here?" I asked, sliding my hand over the rough patch of burned skin on his side as we walked. It was covered now, but it was impossible to miss when he had his shirt off.

"Club loyalty." Mason's expression darkened. He obviously didn't want to talk about it.

"Oh," I replied, trying to think of something to change the subject but failing.

"You know a lot about me," he said after a few agonizingly long minutes. "Tell me a little about yourself."

"What do you want to know?" I asked, feeling a little anxious about what I should actually share with him.

"Well, for starters," he began with a hard smirk, "I guess I'm curious as to how the hell you thought it was a good idea to come after a dangerous criminal in one of the most notorious violent biker gangs in the country."

"Yeah, not my smartest decision." I groaned. Hearing it out loud like that made it sound like the boneheaded idea it was. "In my defense, I wasn't thinking straight at the time. My whole life was crashing down."

"I'm willing to bet that Kenneth prick had something to do with it." Mason's face darkened again.

"Something like that." I thought about glossing over the details and deflecting with some vague answers, but that felt so wrong. Mason had opened himself up to me. As painful as it was to relive, I had to do the same with him.

I sighed, steadied myself, and began.

# Chapter 11
## ELISHA



"I'm in position," John, one of our part-timers, said through the headsets.

This part always made my heart race the fastest. This was why I got into this profession.

"Counting off. Ten, nine, eight…" Once Kenneth, my fiancé, reached five, he stopped counting. After that we all counted in our heads. Kenneth stood opposite me on the other side of the door. He smiled at me the way he always did right before we raided a house. The rockiness and unease between us disappeared. It always did when we were on the porch of someone housing a fugitive.

It struck me as funny—not *ha ha* funny, of course. In an odd way, this was the best version of us. Guns in hand on the precipice of capturing a criminal. This was absolute trust and teamwork. This was when our relationship shined the brightest.

His tall, athletic frame coiled with tension as he stepped into the doorway. The spring air was already starting to heat up. The sunlight refracted off the sweat that beaded down the side of his face. It reminded me of fireflies on a great brown mahogany.

Kenneth held up and retracted his fingers one by one. *Three, two, one.* He took a deep breath and pointed at me.

"Go, go, go!" I shouted over the headset.

Kenneth kicked in the front door, and John kicked in the back. I was right behind Kenneth. He cleared the room to the right, and I cleared the room to the left.

"Mr. Marcus Tenneman," I called out while sweeping the next room. "C'mon out. We have a warrant for your arrest."

Through the kitchen, I saw John testing the bathroom door when it exploded out at him. Our fugitive, Tenneman, shouldered through it as he bolted for the back door. John was thrown headfirst into a China cabinet.

I immediately made my way to him. He was on one knee and was peppered with glass and fine cuts. Dazed but still conscious, he waved us by. "I'm okay. I'm okay."

Kenneth ran after the fugitive. I checked John again just to make sure, then joined my fiancé on the pursuit. I rounded the corner and made a beeline for the back door.

I was barely through the kitchen threshold when I was blindsided by a baseball bat. The back of my vest absorbed most of the blow, but it launched me to the ground. More importantly, the strike knocked my gun out of my hand.

Lying on my stomach, I screamed for Kenneth. He glanced back at me and frowned. The weight of the decision marred his face. It was me or the quickly fleeing bounty.

"John, help Eli!" Kenneth yelled back, then turned away

to chase Tenneman.

I was devastated.

The fugitive's girlfriend stood over me, cursing in Spanish. She was a stout Latina with a mean swing, and she was very angry. John had struggled to his feet, but with the first step forward, he collapsed again. Blood poured from a cut on his forehead. He was more disoriented than he thought. He wouldn't be able to help me.

I was on my own.

I twisted away from the next strike, the bat racking the tile my head had rested on not a second before. The crazy lady reared up for another swing when she saw my gun. She dropped the bat and went for it.

Everything was happening so fast. Dread gripped me. My chest contracted. I could feel my asthma flaring. If she got to my gun….

My father was a cop in a difficult time and place. I always looked up to him for that. I asked him once if he ever got scared when doing his job. He told me that "Fear and courage go hand in hand. It's which one you let take over in tough situations that defines you."

The Latina picked up my gun. I forced my chest to relax and set aside my useless fear. When my adrenaline kicked in and forced me to act, I chose courage.

I slid my Taser out of its holster and fired before she could get my safety off. Her thick form went rigid, then dropped backward like a wooden plank. Wasting no time, I scuttled across the floor and wrenched my gun from her hand. Then I cuffed her.

I exhaled in relief, forcing my heart to slow its galloping pace. That could've gone really bad. I scanned for Kenneth, frowning when I realized he was long gone. *Why do I keep putting up with his shit?*

I helped John up, and after a few minutes, he was all right to walk. We locked the angry girlfriend in the back seat of my SUV and waited for Kenneth by John's car. Kenneth and I had taken my vehicle and John had followed us.

John sat in the passenger seat of his own car. I knew right away that I'd have to drive him back. Most of his wounds were minor, but he was definitely concussed. Blood bloomed like a rose from a slice over his brow. It streamed down his face, closing one of his eyes. I'd need to stitch him up before all the color drained from his pasty freckled skin. I had the full kit back at the office. He'd survive until then.

Kenneth was all smiles and puffed chest when he dragged the man he was chasing to the car.

I tried to maintain my professionalism, but my patience dwindled with each step Kenneth took. "What the hell were you thinking?"

"I was thinking that that was fifty thousand dollars hauling ass away from us." Kenneth was completely unfazed by my tone. He put the fugitive in the back seat with the woman who almost put me in the hospital. They immediately started shouting in Spanish. The cacophony of insults was muffled by the slammed door. "We spent months tracking that—"

"What's this *we* nonsense?" I interrupted. "*I* spent months chasing leads. *I* called all those people, and *I* was the one to stake out the address for a week."

"Yeah, and *I* caught him. See, we're a team, babe—Elisha." He caught himself. I hated being called pet names while on the job. Not that I was fond of them to begin with.

I eyed Kenneth. "You're so busy playing the hotshot that you almost let me and John get hurt or worse!"

"C'mon, Eli. I knew you were strong enough to handle her. And shit, I was right. Look at you. You're fine, and *she's* cuffed in the back seat." Kenneth put on his smooth smile. It used to melt my heart, but now the apparent placation of it all just made me angrier. "I believed in you. I love you, and I knew you'd be all right."

He grabbed my hand and rubbed my arm, trying to pull me in to him. Stubbornly, I held my ground. It was all I could do not to outright pull away. I was still extremely upset at him.

I groaned when I saw the blue and red lights wash over every glass surface in the neighborhood. Neither of us called the police, but it was only a matter of time till they eventually showed up. This was a residential area, after all. I was hoping we'd be gone by then. I'd had my fill with Lawrence County law enforcement.

"I know, Eli. I'll be quick." Kenneth kissed me on the cheek. "Promise." He waved them down.

I recognized a few of the officers who got out of the car to shake Kenneth's hand. They were the same ones who'd made my life miserable at the academy several years back. I could never prove it, but I knew some of them had a hand in my "disqualification."

Two white guys put us through the motions, checking our paperwork. The same way they always did. They tapped on the back seat window and congratulated Kenneth on yet another great catch. He boasted modestly, making sure to sprinkle in some tattered compliments my way as well.

I smiled politely.

That was the best he was getting out of me. Kenneth used to lecture me about letting the past be the past. He would tell me that we needed to make friends with them so they wouldn't harass us every step of the way. The money was good, and the bail bondsmen in the area always called us first, so maybe he was right.

That didn't mean I had to like it.

Kenneth was telling a story about a fugitive we chased into a pool and how the man couldn't swim. We had to pull him out with a child's toy, one of those long foam noodles. It was funny the first dozen times I heard him tell it, but not anymore. Now it was tedious and a time suck.

I could only maintain my strained half smile for so long. "I'm going to bring John back to the office and patch him up."

"Yeah, that sounds good, babe." He tore himself away from the story to wave. "I'll process this guy."

*Babe.*

It stung my ears like an off chord as I walked to John's car. It was hard enough to be taken seriously in this line of work without him calling me pet names in front of the cops. I climbed in the car and told myself that Kenneth's slip of the tongue wasn't intentional.

*He just forgot.*
*Again.*

* * * *

After an inquiry about John, Kenneth wouldn't answer any of my texts. I wish I could claim that was out of the ordinary, but it wasn't. Whenever we brought in a sizable bounty, he'd go to a bar with his cop buddies. I used to get invited, but they mostly ignored me while I was there, so I stopped going.

Normally I wouldn't bother texting him and just let him do his thing, but Kenneth had taken my SUV to process the two people we caught and start the paperwork on our bounty. Sometimes he celebrated a little too much and had to take a taxi home. The thought of my vehicle left in some random parking lot all night long made me anxious.

I was texting him because I didn't know which bar he was at. He and his buddies rotated every week or so, and I didn't feel like barhopping to find him. John saw my frustration and told me which one it was most likely to be tonight. He used to be a regular with the group, but he'd stopped drinking with Kenneth several months ago due to some fight they had. Their relationship these days was strictly professional.

I spotted my SUV right away when my Uber drove us into the parking lot. I got out and tested my door. Unlocked. Of course it was.

"Dammit, Kenneth," I growled. He'd soured my mood by not answering, and now to find my door unlocked? I had my own set of keys, so I could have just taken it right then and driven home. Only I couldn't, not before I gave him a piece of my mind. If I didn't, I'd be up all night fuming.

With the huge dance floor and jumping music, the bar was more of a club. Each of the building's four massive rooms had their own themed bars and wildly different patrons. Honestly, it was kind of a neat setup. One room had line dancing, the next had a live rock band, the one after that was all hip-hop, and then finally a Latin room with some banging salsa fusion music. If I'd been in a better mood and wasn't so exhausted, I might have actually stayed for a drink.

But tonight wasn't the night.

I'd searched for almost an hour, working my way through the throng of people. Kenneth was still nowhere to be found.

There was a glass of wine and a bath calling my name, and to live out that fantasy, I needed to find my damn fiancé. The fact that he wasn't answering me and that I hadn't found him yet was getting me really heated.

And that's when I saw *her* car.

Across the street in the motel parking lot was Chelsea's bright pink Prius. I told myself it was just a coincidence. Our receptionist just happened to be in the same area as my fiancé, that was all.

Just a coincidence.

My throat dried out, and a pit began to form in my stomach as I walked over to it. It was the same feeling I had a few years ago when I found Kenneth in bed with one of my girlfriends.

He promised it would never happen again. It was difficult, but eventually we worked through it. We'd been dating since high school, and he was all I really knew when it came to partners. Then last year, fresh out of college, we started this bounty hunting business together. Between our house and our business, we were tied to one another in so many ways now. I desperately wanted to give him the benefit of the doubt.

It was just a coincidence.

The blinds were drawn, of course, but I still heard a soft moan through the door. I seized up. Part of me screamed to run away. To trust in Kenneth and assume that if Chelsea was in there, she was with some other man.

I couldn't do that.

If I did, then every time I looked at either of them, there would be a nagging doubt. It would poison the very foundation of our relationship. I couldn't live like that.

My hand shook as I grasped the doorknob and turned. That too was unlocked. The door drifted open noiselessly. The first thing I saw was Kenneth's jacket on the chair. After that, strewn across the floor, were the rest of their clothes.

Right then my heart knew the truth, but it was my mind and eyes that needed the confirmation. The door was pushed ever wider by numb limbs that moved automatically. Through the mirror opposite the bed, I saw two brown swatches entangled atop a cream comforter.

It was them.

My eyes fell to the engagement ring Kenneth had given me after he cheated on me the first time. My hand was shaking so badly that I almost couldn't get the damn diamond-studded ring off my finger. When I finally did, the silver band felt toxic. For a moment I watched them, hoping they'd notice me.

When they did, I would fling open the door and throw the ring in his lying, cheating face. Then I would curse at them and storm out.

Maybe it was because of the empty champagne bottles or the fact that he thought he'd locked the door, but they never once looked up. The longer I stood in that doorway, the sicker I felt. All my cherished truths began to fray at their ends.

A hollowness formed in me that carved out my insides. I wanted to scream or cry, but neither came. I dropped the ring on the striped maroon and peach carpet, then closed the door behind me.

I walked back to my SUV with the solemnness of a funeral procession. It wasn't a person I was leaving behind this time but an entire life. No. It was worse than that. I had buried the only future I'd ever imagined.

After driving around for an hour, I found myself at our office. Going home seemed wrong. The thought of going back to our house and the bed we shared made me physically nauseous. I needed to occupy my mind, bury it in something productive before I made myself ill. So I drove to work instead.

I locked my SUV and went inside the stout U-shaped brick building. This late at night, the third-floor offices that we rented were dark and lonely. I was glad for it. The last thing I wanted was any kind of small talk.

Kenneth and I had separate offices. We decided early on that personal space was a necessity if we were going to work together. His door was shut, so I was spared his lingering presence, but not Chelsea's. The other employees shared a common area.

Chelsea's desk squatted directly between our two offices. It was impossible to pass by without being assaulted by her perfume and personal effects. Happy pictures of her oblivious husband and kids littered her desk with hypocrisy.

What did she tell them? Did she say she had to work late? I bet she did.

I wanted to sweep an arm across it all and knock everything onto the floor.

Although restraint pained me, I was too much of a professional for something like that.

I slammed my office door instead. That much I could do. I was betrayed and upset, not only at Kenneth but at myself too. I'd tied myself to a liar so completely that the amount of things we'd cosigned on made my head spin.

What was I going to do now?

A sense of impotent rage washed over me. I slammed my palm onto my desk and screamed. I was listless and hopeless, like I was floating on a raft in the open sea, watching distant lights blink out one by one.

My strike knocked a basket of files onto the floor. They were the bounties we reviewed and declined. Some of them weren't feasible while others weren't worth enough to make a profit on.

And some, like the first folder I picked up—a Mr. Mason Mason Stone—were just too dangerous. Kenneth decided against that one before I got the chance to review it. He was doing too much of that lately.

There was a mugshot-style thumbnail picture clipped to the outside of the folder.

Mr. Stone was surprisingly cute for a criminal.

*Mason Mason*? Weird that he'd have two identical first names. I wondered if it was some sort of filing error. I flipped it over. The point of origin was a small town in North Carolina. That explained it. Small towns had a terrible tendency of misfiling, omitting, or outright losing information.

That might've been another reason Kenneth declined this bounty.

I turned on my computer and checked the North Carolina database. Mr. Stone, first name Mason, was still in there, and the bounty was indeed active. That was it, though. Usually there was a lot more information about the fugitive. There was only one lead noted: 'Presumed association with the outlaw motorcycle club *the Broken Veins*.'

That was probably the real reason why Kenneth didn't want to follow up on it. Biker gangs were incredibly violent, especially one-percenters like the Broken Veins. I skimmed the file. Throughout his life, Mason had apparently been arrested several times, but the charges had all been redacted.

*Weird.* I read on. Most of the charges were dropped when he was in his midtwenties.

Still, North Carolina definitely wanted him. They were

willing to pay a staggering five hundred thousand dollars!

*Jesus, what did this Mason guy do?* I'd seen fugitives on the run from nasty felonies and the bounty was half as much. I checked the site again and would call tomorrow just to make absolutely sure.

I'd never taken a bounty on my own before, let alone one this dangerous. I knew I shouldn't go for it, but I needed an excuse not to be around for a few days, and the rest of the bounties in the basket were all too small.

Besides, could I really pass up that kind of money?

I looked around my tiny room. The framed vacation photo stood on the edge of my desk and stared back at me. It was from when Kenneth and I went to Hawaii. 'Together forever' read the text around the border. I pushed it off my desk in disgust and felt a cathartic release when the glass shattered against the floor.

*Fuck you, Kenneth.*

Holding Mason's folder was empowering. It felt like I was taking my life back into my own hands.

I tucked the folder under my arm and left the building. I'd rather surround myself with vicious bikers than be stuck in this office with Kenneth and Chelsea. Five hundred thousand dollars could buy me out of this lie of a life. I could move away and start over. A fresh start was only one criminal away.

How could I not chase that dream?

# Chapter 12
## ELISHA

I had been floating all morning after another steamy session with Mason had us fucking all over the hotel room. I felt bad for the cleaning crew; there wasn't a surface in that whole room that we didn't at least bump into during our circuitous route to the shower.

The only thing that took away from my glow as I made my way down to the hotel lobby for the breakfast spread was the nagging reminder that we'd used the last condom last night. We desperately tried to do the right thing, but neither of us could resist. Mason pulled out as he came, but… well, there was always the possibility that he wasn't fast enough.

I tried to put the concern out of my mind, at least until after Mason's meeting tonight. *One train wreck at a time.*

When I came back into our hotel room, I heard Mason on the phone with his handler. He wore the same serious, disdainful expression every time he talked to Harris. Even with a full tray from the breakfast buffet, I was able to quietly close the door behind me.

It must've been so difficult to operate under the thumb of such ruthless organizations. I had no idea how Mason was able to keep it together. I couldn't imagine what it must be like to know your bosses considered you to be an expendable asset. They thought of him as a paper towel, something to be used to clean up a mess and then discarded.

The sickening thing was that it wasn't just the biker gang that dehumanized him, it was our own government. How could they use him like that?

My father was a police officer, and I'd have been one too if circumstances were different. I'd always known there was inherent corruption and racism in police departments, but I'd never given much thought to what happened on the federal level.

It was completely legal, but what the FBI was doing to Mason *felt* criminal.

I set the tray down on the small table and blew on my coffee to cool it. My problems seemed so small in comparison. Sure, Mason agreed to this, but I could tell he didn't know what he was getting himself into. Freedom was an intoxicating thing. To have it all around you and still be trapped must've felt awful.

"Yes, I got it. I'll drop it off this time, just give me the address of the gym," Mason replied impatiently. "I'll pick up the fresh recorder on the way. Just make sure you get me out when you have enough. Don't fuck me on this, Harris." He hung up.

I no longer felt the need to scrutinize his every move and conversation. I trusted him now. I couldn't place exactly when the transition happened, but I'd like to think it didn't have anything to do with the sex. Although the tenderness in the way he held me did make me feel safer than I'd ever been.

I think it was after the attack by the bikers. Even after I raised the gun on him, he believed in me when no sane person should have. The things I put him through for the sake of a misfiled bounty, and my own greed, were monstrous. I still felt bad every time I saw the bandage on his wrist from the cuffs.

Why did Mason save me when all I was doing was making things worse for him?

If he'd let the Broken Veins do… whatever they were going to do to me, then they would completely trust him. Everything would've been so much easier for him. He wouldn't have to worry about getting a knife in the back or a bullet through the side of his head.

How could I not trust him fully now?

Mason might've been the only person I could trust these days. It was a crazy feeling, both scary and liberating. My savior, my tarnished knight, was a criminal, an outlaw. I knew I could leave any time I wanted to, but I was falling too damn hard.

That was the scariest part of all of this.

When I sat next to him on the bed, his giant hand drifted over to my thigh and squeezed it tightly. I marveled at the contrast of the light on dark flesh tones, and still couldn't fully believe this whole thing had actually happened.

"Everything all right?" I handed him a coffee.

"That a trick question?" He snorted a weak chuckle and removed his hand from my leg. I immediately felt a longing for his pressure to return. He took a sip of the scalding liquid. "Everything is at least going to plan. For now."

Mason looked back at me with soft eyes. I could see a distant sadness in them when he pushed out his breath. Something heavy weighed on him. What had his handler said to him?

I was going to rephrase my question when, like a sudden raincloud, his expression grew real dark.

"The meeting got pushed up," he said. "I have to head out."

Mason stood up and snatched his vest off a chair.

"Right now?" The words came out automatically. It was a knee-jerk question to a cruel answer I already knew.

"Stay off your phone, and don't talk to anyone." He paused, and there was something in his features that terrified me. It was the look I imagined firefighters had when they went into an especially bad burning building. "If I'm not back by midnight, then I'm not.... If you don't see me by then, you need to get the hell out of here."

*That's it?*

My ribs were a house of cards set to topple. The notion that he might not be coming back collapsed my insides with dread. My heart did frantic laps in my chest. My airways constricted, which drove my hands to unconsciously reach for the bump of my inhaler in my pocket.

I forced myself to calm, but my mind still raced. Was this really the end?

No. I couldn't let him leave without knowing.

"Have you given any thought to what happens after all this?" I asked timidly. "With us?"

Mason slipped on his leather, the physical and emotional armor that protected him. The oiled, patched-up black vest looked so out of place in this nice, modern hotel room. It looked out of place in my life as a whole.

In my *old* life.

He walked to the bed and towered over me, softly caressing my cheek. I stood up to meet him despite my legs suddenly becoming almost too weak to stand. Mason kissed me with the same intensity that encapsulated the rest of our short time together.

I reached for a second kiss, *just one more,* but he'd already turned away.

It was too abrupt. We should've had more time. We didn't even have a chance to see what could've been. The whole thing was obscenely unfair. We'd gone through too much to not at least get a proper goodbye.

His face went stone stern as he made for the door. He pushed it open and lingered in the threshold, not daring to look as he said one word. It was short and cruel and cut worse than any knife ever could.

"No," he said.

And then he was gone.

The next several hours were hell. I cried a lot. I relived the parting in agonizing detail, and then came the crashing waves of doubt.

He was trying to make me hate him, but it was too late

for that. I refused to believe he didn't care about me. There was more to it than that. There had to be. He was just playing the part, wasn't he? Trying to keep me safe by pushing me away?

I desperately wanted to go with him, help him in some way. But I knew how impossible that was, with him being undercover and having to portray this vulgar biker character. It was all just an act for him. He didn't mean it.

I hoped I was right about Mason.

The one dominating emotion that made all my insignificant problems fall by the wayside was worry. I was devastated by the loss of the foolish fantasy that we might end up together, but even more than that, I wanted Mason to be all right.

I'd seen firsthand what these monsters were capable of. I shuddered to think what they would do to him if they found out he was a rat. All I could do now was hope and pray.

I needed him to come back to me.

The breakfast had long since cooled, left untouched on the table. I couldn't eat anything. I was worrying myself sick. I needed a distraction.

I'd left my phone charger at the motel in Carver, so my cell had been dead for a while. I called the front desk, and they brought me an old charger from lost and found. Mason's warning still rang clearly in my head. I wasn't planning on calling anyone, just distracting myself with the internet for a few hours.

When the phone eventually turned on, I saw I had several voice mails. Looking through my call history, I saw that some of them were from the police. They were probably notifying me that they found my SUV.

The vast majority of the others were from Kenneth.

Several minutes later, he called again. I muted the ring and let it go to voice mail. Had he been calling me all day?

I hated when he got obsessive like this. All his texts basically boiled down to "Where are you?" And "We need to talk." And "Call me back now!"

*Not likely.*

A little while later, he called again. I turned the phone off, not wanting to deal with the constant barrage. Kenneth could wait until tomorrow, or the rest of my life. I hadn't decided yet.

I was emotionally and physically exhausted. I didn't remember falling asleep on the bed, or how long I was out for.

But I'd never forget how I woke up.

There was a rapid tapping on the door. I thought I might have way overslept and management was coming to kick me out. Darkness blanketed the room from the partially drawn curtains. The sun had gone down.

"Coming," I called out. My head was pounding from disorientation and a raging headache.

How long had I slept for?

The incessant tapping continued.

"Okay, okay, I'm coming." I stretched and rubbed some of the sleep from my eyes. I walked to the peephole and peered through. It was a young, red-haired cleaning lady. At first glance, I thought the pale Irish girl looked upset. Then I took a closer look and saw it for what it actually was.

Fear.

A pit formed in my stomach, churning with impossible possibilities. I crept back and grabbed my gun, just in case. I only opened the door to the length of the security chain. I began to speak. "Yes, what—"

Before I could get the rest of the question out, the door was kicked in. The flimsy chain exploded around me as I was thrown to the floor. Instinctively I went to raise the gun, but I didn't have a clear shot. Whoever was there was using the maid as a shield.

Tears streamed down her cheeks as a pistol was pointed at me from over her shoulder. "Ah ah ah," the voice teased. The man motioned for me to toss away my gun.

It pained me to throw away my only defense, but I did it. What other option did I have? I wasn't going to shoot through the poor girl. Now that I wasn't a threat, the maid was shoved into the room beside me.

Four men strode in, all with the same familiar vests and designs. The Broken Veins had finally found me.

The man with the gun had a broad, sweeping smile that was half covered by his bushy push-broom mustache. It was his eyes that made me realize who he was and just how much danger I was in.

I remembered them from the file and from Mason's description earlier.

Double D's eyes were a cold, vivid blue and filled to the brim with sadistic glee. He let the room's door, my only escape, softly click shut behind him.

This was the man who'd smashed my windows when I captured Mason. He almost killed me back then, but with Mason's help, I was able to slip away. Now there was no place for me to run.

And no Mason here to help me.

Without my gun, I was completely at their mercy.

By staying with Mason, I'd been playing with fire. Deep down, I think I always knew I would get burned. I just thought it would be Mason who would do the burning.

For as scared as I was, I at least knew what was happening. The poor maid had no idea what was going on. She just wanted to go home to her family. The terror on her face made her already light complexion turn a ghostly white. She had to be around my age, but the frightened innocence on her features made her look even younger.

The maid kicked over the small black waste can in an attempt to shuffle away from the giant bikers. It drew the attention of Double D. Her eyes flashed, then twinkled, pleading with the man. *'I'll do anything,'* her green eyes seemed to say, *'just don't hurt me!'*

Without any hesitation, the Broken Veins' president drew his gun and shot the maid in the forehead. A chunky, bright red mist sprayed the wall and my abandoned breakfast.

I didn't realize I was even screaming until the smoking gun was pointed at me. The smile fading from beneath his mustache, Double D looked at me intently. He was weighing my usefulness, deciding whether I would live or die.

Finally, he clicked the hammer of his pistol out of the firing position and slid the gun away. He turned, opening

the room's door.
    "Take her."

# Chapter 13
## MASON

I walked into the Anytime Fitness like I'd done hundreds of times over the past two years. Granted, I'd never been to this one in Little Rock, Arkansas, before, but it didn't matter. They were generally all the same all across the country; that's why the FBI got me my membership.

I'd never worked out before I went to prison. Truth be told, running a stolen car stripping and selling empire made me kind of soft, all things considered. I'd spend most of my day on the phone, online, or managing spreadsheets, and most of my nights getting fucked up with—then fucked by—all the girls who always found their way to powerful men. I had a nice place with a big pool and more drugs than a pharmacy, and it was always full of gorgeous women. My only real exercise regimen was pounding pussy, and maybe twenty minutes on my elliptical when I wasn't too hungover. Of course, I was rarely not too hungover....

That all changed when I got to prison, but not as much as you'd think. Being trapped in a cell smaller than my old walk-in closet was a huge departure from my cocaine-fueled big-swinging-dick lifestyle. I lifted weights mostly to stave off the boredom of staring at the fucking walls.

When I took the deal to become an informant, the first thing the FBI did, even before finding me housing, was get me a membership to one of the biggest gym franchises in the country. I went to the gym four times a week, not because I wanted to but because I *had* to.

The automatic doors opened, and I was hit with the familiar muted smell of fresh sweat being covered by antiseptic cleaning supplies. It was a smell I found I didn't mind, actually. I nodded to the staff at the front desk, and when they scanned my card, they politely welcomed me to Arkansas. With all the anxiety I had about the coming meet with Ratchet and the constant din of worry surrounding my ongoing relationship with the feds, I wanted nothing more than to knock out a few sets, but I didn't have the time for that.

When I got into the locker room, I splashed some cold water on my face and started getting into character.

"Yippee ki yay, motherfucker," I muttered to myself, staring intently at my dripping face in their wall of mirrors. "Time to get to work."

I searched the lockers for the one my handlers always used. That's how this worked. They came to the gym a day before me, left a fresh recorder safely locked away, and then swung by a day after to pick up the spent one. The combination changed every week, but that was easy enough to memorize.

Lifting weights was actually just my cover for the club.

It was an easy sell with the macho assholes in my chapter. Hell, sometimes they even lifted with me. All the while they had no idea why I was really there.

This time though, something was incredibly wrong. Regardless of the gym, the FBI always used the same locker—the bottommost left one that was available. Only now for the first time in two years, it was empty. No lock, no recorder, no notes, *nothing*.

I frantically searched all the lockers and still nothing

After several forced breaths to calm down, I went outside and called Harris.

"Where the fuck is my new recorder?" I asked in hushed tones in an empty, shaded area of the parking lot.

"I was just about to text you. You're not getting a new one. Things have changed," Harris said dismissively on speakerphone. I heard him distractedly rifling through some paperwork.

"The fuck do you mean, things have changed? I'm on my way to the annual right now."

"Yeah, you're now on hold until the next meeting," he replied between sips of something and giving someone else a few short commands.

"The next meeting isn't for another full year. That's why they're called annuals." I fumed quietly. "Who knows if Ratchet will still be in the game then?"

"Look. I don't know what to tell you. Did you see the press conference earlier today? The new director is reassigning most of us to deal with the terrorist attack. All low-priority work is suspended until further notice."

"Low priority?" I nearly coughed at the insanity of what he was saying. "I spent two years gaining the trust to even be invited to—"

"You're just going to have to tough it out until you become a priority again. Keep your head down, and try to stay in tight with—"

"You're really fucking me on this, Harris." I couldn't contain myself. "They're expecting me at the meeting. I don't have the fucking luxury of keeping my head down!"

"Keep your voice down." Harris closed a door, probably to his office, and took me off speakerphone. His tone was quieter and hinted at something other than dismissive disdain for once. "I'll concede that it's a rough break, but you have to understand that you don't matter to us. We're overworked and understaffed here on most operations. I get that your life is on the line here, but so are many others, most of whom aren't criminals."

I exhaled sharply through my nose. My past was going to follow me for the rest of my short life. What the fuck was Elisha going to do? It wasn't like she could pretend to be dead for a full year, and telling Harris about her would break our agreement and immediately put me back in prison.

*Fuck.*

"So what does that mean for me? Now that I'm no longer *important*, am I free to just leave?" I asked. "Is our deal finished?"

The way the club was flushing out informants these days, I wouldn't survive until the next meeting.

"Fuck no. You've got at least another decade of time

owed in prison. You don't get to just walk. We own you until your sentence is up or we *let* you go," he shot back immediately.

"That's bullshit! Two years—"

"And no arrests to show for it," he cut me off, giving me a long pause to let that sink in before continuing. "For now, you're on cruise control. No dedicated handler and no check-ins until we contact you again. Do not get in trouble, because as of now, you will be completely unsupported."

"No support as of now? How exactly is that different than before?"

"Stay useful, Mason," Harris sharply replied, then abruptly hung up.

"You motherfucker!" I screamed into the phone, knowing he couldn't hear me.

I stood alone in the parking lot, vibrating with rage, before I forced myself to think through the situation productively. Appealing to any sense of compassion within Harris was a nonstarter. I had to switch gears and try something else.

*Stay useful.*

One way or another, this had to end today, for Elisha's sake. When word got out that she was still alive, the Broken Veins were going to come after her, if for nothing else than just to clean up loose ends.

*Stay useful.*

Not to mention Double D's growing paranoia and relentless searching for another rat. I sincerely doubted I'd make it another full year without being found out. If not that, then by the time the next annual rolled around, I'd no doubt need to have committed a serious crime to stay in the club. When I did that, it wouldn't matter if the feds found out or not. All my worst fears would've come true. I'd have truly become one of them—a Broken Vein.

What would Elisha think of me then?

*Stay useful.* Harris's last words annoyingly ran in circles in my mind. I kept dismissing it because he was such an asshole, but what if he was right?

I pulled out the small recorder I was going to drop off. Like all the rest of them I turned in, this one had some incriminating conversations on it, but not enough to put away anyone outside my chapter. If the whole club wasn't a federal priority at the moment, then Double D and his goons sure as hell weren't either.

What if I went through with the assignment anyway?

I pulled the recorder out of my pocket and rolled it between my fingers. It was no larger than a USB thumb drive. And this one still had memory and battery for several more hours of evidence taping.

That still might not be enough. I needed to make the Broken Veins and their connections to the gun cartels matter on the main stage.

How the hell was I going to do that?

Then it came to me.

The enemy of my enemy….

"He wants me to stay useful, huh?" I pushed my tongue against the back row of my teeth, then cracked my neck on both sides. "Okay."

*When the game is rigged, you gotta stop playing by their rules.*

# Chapter 14
## MASON

The paved road to Castor Farm ended under a canopy of arching trees and gave way to a well-traveled dirt path that led to a massive field. That was where the annual was held every year.

Middle-of-fucking-nowhere, Arkansas.

Phil Castor was one of the original Steel Veins back in the day. He wasn't too pleased with the abrupt shift in leadership, so when the club splintered off into the Broken Veins, he was quick to jump ship with them. After he died, the Castor family opened it up to the Broken Veins for as long as we wanted it. The farm was on a remote stretch of land just outside Little Rock, perfectly secluded from any neighbors.

It was great for us, but not for the Castors. With all the wreckage the annual caused every year, I had no idea why they kept honoring the agreement. They were probably too scared to call it off.

The first thing that caught my eye when the copse of trees opened up was the raging fire. It was just a wood fire for now, but it was still fairly early. Soon, some prospect would drive a beater bike or stolen car through the inferno for the crowd's entertainment.

It was an insane rite of passage.

The burns on my back and side itched at the memory of my fiery ride. Double D wasn't looking when I did my ride, so he made me go through again. When I caught fire the second time through, they put me out with beer. I was patched into the club that night.

Slowly riding in, I passed a few parked supply vans and a sixty-person charter bus. They held all the food, booze, tents, women, supplies, and everything else that couldn't make the trip on two wheels.

When I parked my bike, I saw the field party was full tilt. Topless girls pushed around ice pits, which were just wheelbarrows filled with ice and booze. The prospects hadn't finished setting up the firing range yet, but that didn't stop full patch members from letting a few shots fly over their heads to speed them up. Another gunshot signaled the beginning of the first slow race of the evening, where members tried to get their motorcycles to the finish line as slowly as possible without putting their feet on the ground.

The whole thing reminded me of Burning Man, only one that was a hundred times more dangerous.

Tents of all types and sizes dotted the field with no specific layout or consistency. The uniform boxy black tents were the exception. Those were the business tents, little mobile chapels for each chapter of the club.

No one was allowed to fuck with those tents.

I had a little time before my meeting with Ratchet, so I grabbed a beer from one of the rolling ice pits and looked for the Philly tent. It was time to bite the bullet and confront Double D and the rest of the boys. I had no idea what I was going to say about the abduction or the killings in Carver. I'd just have to feel them out and go from there.

I searched with slow, weighted steps. My mind was two hours behind me, in a hotel room in Memphis. Elisha's worried voice ran circles in my heart. I felt worse about the way I left things with her than I did about the upcoming life-threatening meeting.

I had to rip that Band-Aid off the way I did, or I wouldn't have been able to leave her at all. There was nowhere I'd rather be than back with her, but how long could we have kept up the lie?

What were we going to do? Just run off together like a pair of lovesick puppies and pretend the world wasn't crashing down all around us? Even if this insane new plan worked, I wasn't going to be riding off into the sunset. I could try to tell myself different, but deep down I knew that wasn't how my story was going to end.

Elisha and I didn't have a chance. We'd never carve out our piece of the American dream or grow old together. Fuck, I'd be surprised if I grew old enough to see tomorrow.

It was a wonderful lie while it lasted.

I could rationalize it all I wanted, but the truth was I just missed her.

No one could find her unless she did something stupid, and I was confident that she was too smart for that. Despite everything between us, knowing she was safe made all the difference. It freed me up to worry about the task at hand instead.

"Slag," I called out to one of our prospects. He was carrying a plastic folding table into our black tent. It would serve as our chapter's meeting table for the weekend.

"Shiiiiit. I'm sorry it's not set up yet, Cowboy." Slag put the table down. "Ginge told me you were all making a detour and wouldn't be back for a while."

"Detour? What fucking detour?" Considering all they'd done to come after me and their suspicions about my loyalty, what could possibly detour them? Was I just being paranoid?

Maybe they didn't suspect me of being a rat after all.

"Yeah, bro." Slag had the slight wobble about him that came with being as high as he was. "I thought I had more time, so y'know, I blazed up with Illinois guys." He smiled wide as if remembering a really funny joke. "They've got this killer weed they say only grows on top of their mountains—"

"There are no mountains in Illinois, dumbass." I shook my head. "Tell me about the detour, Slag. Where'd they go?"

He pursed his lips together, then shrugged.

It wasn't his fault, not really. Members never gave prospects anything but orders. They were good little soldiers, just following orders.

I looked out over the organized chaos of the annual. When it all came crashing down, that ignorance might be the only thing that saved them.

But I doubted it.

Slag asked me something as I walked away, but I didn't hear nor respond to it. I was already calling our pres to find out what was going on. I needed to get a feel for the climate of my chapter before I met Ratchet. If they shared any of their concerns with him, I was fucked. All I'd get out of the coming meeting would be a bullet.

No answer from Double D. I then tried Ginge, our monstrous sergeant-at-arms. Again, nothing. I tried calling the rest, but their phones were either on silent or went to voice mail.

I doubted they were deliberately ignoring me. It was pretty common for them not to hear or bother with answering while they were riding. Hearing a ringtone or differentiating between a vibrating phone and the hum of a motorcycle was also damn near impossible on a bike. That made sense to me, but it did little to quiet that growing unease I felt rolling around in the pit of my stomach.

I needed them here for what came next.

For years I'd lived on the razor's edge, knowing someday a gentle breeze would topple me one direction or another.

A moment of panic welled up in me. I'd have to go in blind, having no idea what Ratchet knew about me or my chapter. A small, consistent voice in my head screamed at me. *Get the fuck out of there! Go get Elisha and make a run for it!*

Yeah, and while I was at it, I'd fly into space and take a bite out of the moon.

*I'm here to do a job,* I reminded myself, straightening

my posture. I was too close to the end to not see it through. I drained the rest of my mostly full beer in big gulps, hoping to drown that scared, doubtful voice that welled up within me.

Easily spotting Ratchet's chapter's tent, I slid a cigarette from the pack I kept in my vest pocket and made my way over. I lit it, letting it hang from my lip in the usual way as I asked one of his guys for his whereabouts.

I never smoked before joining the Broken Veins, but I had to pick up the habit. The most important club business was discussed over a cigarette on a smoke break. Always keeping a pack on me had been my ticket to secretly record those conversations.

I'd have figured the meeting would've been in the black tent, but I was wrong. They pointed me to a private RV toward the tree line.

I was greeted by a pair of burly prospects outside Ratchet's trailer. They stopped me when I tried to go in. "We gotta frisk you," one of them told me after an apology. His hands were out and ready.

"Like hell you are." The cigarette fell from my lips as I slapped his slow, fat hands down. I shoved him up against the aluminum-sided trailer and watched as the other prospect backed off.

Making sure I was mic'd up appropriately was old hat for me considering how many times I'd done it for the feds, but now there was an additional wrinkle. I made a pit stop before pulling in and met with the enemy of my enemy. In addition to my personal recorder, my *new* partner gave me another small bug which would let them listen in real time to what was being discussed.

Being that I was the only one who had any real skin in the game, if I was caught before the meeting even started, they'd probably leave me to the wolves. There was no guarantee that they'd even come for me if this whole thing went tits up. I had to get them what they wanted *before* they were willing to ride in as the cavalry.

The only hand I had to play was that of indignation. How dare they harass a full-blown patch member.

"You see these patches, motherfucker?" I pulled at the corner of my vest, raising my insignia. "It says 'get your goddamn hands off me.'"

The RV door swung open and a smooth, dusky voice rang out from inside. "What's all the racket?" Ratchet leaned out just far enough to rest against the frame. He looked down at us and scratched the stubble on his chin.

"Fucking TSA out here is trying to fondle my shit." I snapped an annoyed look at Ratchet. "I thought you invited me here for a meeting, not a hand job."

"What's gotten you all fired up, Cowboy?" Ratchet asked. He was balding, of medium build, and soft in the middle. If he were better dressed, he wouldn't look out of place at an accounting firm.

"Since when the fuck do we pat down members?"

"Since a multimillion-dollar deal was on the table. Can't be too careful these days. The Broken Veins aren't as tight as they used to be." There was an edge to his stare as he locked eyes with me. "I heard your chapter has an infestation problem."

He was referring to Swift, the other guy in our club who was an informant, apparently. Or at least I hoped he was referring to Swift.

"*Had* an infestation problem," I said, referring to what happened to Swift when we found out. "I dealt with that personally. We're whole now."

Ratchet's gaze drifted. He nodded slowly, scratching his chin again.

"Good to see you boys still know how to regulate." His eyes snapped back up at me. The redness of his northern European heritage seemed to make his face glow in the sunless overcast day.

"Still gotta frisk you. Don't worry, they won't take your stash or anything." He paused, then asked, "It's not like you have anything to hide, right?"

I saw in his eyes that he wasn't going to budge. This was going to happen whether I was insulted or not. If I protested any more or even walked away, not only would I not get what I needed, but I'd also look very suspicious. I needed to find a way not to lose face.

"I paid my dues," I grumbled, peeling up the fabric on my right side to reveal the burn scars of my fire ride. "If anyone is going to frisk me, I'll be goddamned if it isn't at least another full patch member." I glared at Ratchet's intimidated watchmen. "Not some virgin fucking prospects."

Ratchet eyed me, staying quiet for a long time.

"I can respect that." He nodded, walking down the few steps to first shake my hand.

I held my arms out as the older man patted me down.

*Keep it together,* I reminded myself, putting on a mask of bored confidence as Ratchet went up my legs and then arms, inching ever closer to the device that would get me killed. When he had me take out my wallet, phone, keys, and everything else in my pockets, I realized just how serious he was taking this. With a deal this big, MC brother or not, Ratchet wasn't taking any chances. I couldn't hide a fucking toothpick from his thorough pat down.

It was only a matter of moments now whether I was found out or not.

Throughout it all, I wasn't thinking about the club consequences, or the cavalry abandoning me. Even now, in the fucking thick of it, I was thinking about Elisha and the way I'd left things. I still felt shitty about that, but it was better this way. I'd probably be dead in a few minutes.

I didn't have anything to remember her by, not even a shitty picture on my phone. Although our time together was incredibly short, I'd committed most of her form to memory. Every nuance and curve of her beautiful brown body.

"What's this?" Ratchet asked, patting over the bump in my vest.

*What I wouldn't give to hear her voice one more time.*

Ratchet pulled out my pack of cigarettes and held it up. "I didn't know you smoked." He shook the pack. It was almost full.

"Down to just two a day." I sighed. "They say it's harder to kick than heroin."

"'They' say a lot of things." He bitterly spat the words out.

Ratchet studied the pack intently, almost longingly. "Mostly bullshit."

I read his expression and took a chance.

"Want one?" I asked.

"Fuck yes, I do." He brought the closed pack up to his nose and smelled it, then turned it over in his hands.

Ratchet swallowed hard, then handed the cigarettes back to me as if the pack suddenly got too hot to hold. He pulled down the waistband of his jeans enough to show the top of a white nicotine patch. Turning away, he motioned for me to join him inside. I followed, closing the door to the RV behind me.

"Would it be a dick move if I smoked?" I asked. I'd heard someone say Ratchet was a recovering smoker and decided this was my only play.

It was a hell of a gamble, but it paid off.

"Go ahead." Ratchet shrugged, not bothering to turn to me when he spoke. "Just because I don't smoke anymore doesn't mean I'm not always surrounded by it. Just don't let me touch the damn things, or I'm going to want a drag."

"Thanks." I nodded, carefully opening the pack in a way that he couldn't see inside. The recording devices were blatantly obvious and took up most of the pack. I had them nestled tightly between a ring of cigarettes so the pack would have the right feel to it, but had he opened it, I'd have been fucked.

Pulling out a cigarette and replacing the pack in my breast pocket, I sat on the couch and made myself comfortable.

"I gotta try that nicotine patch," I said, lighting up, then blowing a stream of smoke away from me and Ratchet. "These fucking things will kill you."

I stifled a chuckle at the fact that this time they did the opposite. This time cigarettes saved my life.

We talked for over two hours. Ratchet had heard about my grand theft auto empire back in the day and wanted to recruit me to move guns for a Mexican cartel. We discussed every aspect of the organization in painstaking detail, everything from the vast network of contacts that would need to be cultivated to how we were actually going to physically move the merchandise. It was all laid out on the table.

He laughed and patted me on the back when I suggested we use ambulances as a cover to move the guns into urban areas. The planning came so natural to me, and if I was being honest, there was an aspect to the logistics that I actually missed. Something about all the moving parts and meticulous plans really appealed to me.

The other scary thing was that I saw a lot of myself in Ratchet. It was like looking into a dark mirror. If I hadn't gotten caught by the feds, I might have eventually turned to gunrunning too.

I shook the haunting vision from my mind. This life had a way of getting its hooks into you. But I was different now. It wasn't the feds who were the catalyst for the change in me. Well, maybe on the surface they were. No, it was meeting Elisha that reminded me of the person I could be—*a good man*.

"I'm going to need to know in detail who we're

working with." That was the main point of contention, and also the one thing I desperately needed from Ratchet—the names of his existing partners and cartel contacts.

"Why?" Ratchet crossed his arms and leaned back, looking me over suspiciously.

I raised my eyebrows, frowned, and got up to leave. He stopped me at the door, saying he was willing to share them with me as long as I gave him a good reason to.

"I've been down this road before and don't like where it leads. In my cell, I promised myself to never work with partners I couldn't personally vet. I need to make sure I'm not getting back into bed with any of the motherfuckers who put me in jail last time around."

He eventually agreed. We went through everyone involved, who they were, what their roles were, everything. It was glorious. I was harvesting a gold mine of incriminating evidence. There was enough info here for RICO to destroy the Broken Veins and really put the hurt on the gun cartels.

That was if the feds ever got around to giving a shit about that again.

My cell phone vibrated with the text message I had been waiting for. "This is CVS. Your prescription is ready for pickup," it said. That was the only warning I was going to get from my new partner.

It was code for "we're going to keep our end of the bargain, and you need to get the fuck out of there right now."

They didn't have to tell me twice. The clock was officially ticking on my exit.

The first thing that flashed through my mind was Elisha.

I'd never dreamed the meeting would go this well or that they'd keep their side of the bargain.

*Holy shit, I might actually get to see her again.*

"Good news?" Ratchet asked.

"Huh?" I only then felt the smile that had betrayed me and spread across my lips. I wouldn't have gotten that happy over a prescription, so I decided to just be honest. We were past the part where he might check my phone, so fuck it. "Oh, yeah. It's just this girl I've been seeing lately. Can't seem to get her out of my head."

I guided the conversation to a point where it naturally wound down. Ratchet and I shook hands, promising to meet up when he got word from the cartel, and then I slipped out of there as fast as I could. I beelined to my bike, calculating the time it would take to get back to Memphis if I left right now. Everything else I'd figure out on the way. When I left this morning, I knew it was a crapshoot whether I'd see her again, and I didn't like my odds.

I couldn't believe the Hail Mary I'd just pulled out of my ass. It shouldn't have worked. By now I should've been lying in a pool of my own blood. But here I was.

The only thing that mattered to me now was getting back to that girl and destroying our hotel bed. I had to force my legs to slow down into a casual walking speed so as not to draw unwanted attention.

I didn't have much time left to get off farm property before everything turned into a very different kind of chaos. I was on my bike a few minutes later and back on the paved road a few minutes after that.

Up ahead, barreling toward me, was a small army of bikers. They were strapped with some serious firepower and didn't bother trying to hide it. Semiautomatic rifles and shotguns were slung over their backs, partially concealing the MC insignia boldly printed on each man's vest. I didn't need to read their MC's name to know who they were. Seeing them speeding past me toward the farm with their bulletproof vests, black helmets, and heavy weaponry reminded me of the old kill teams I'd heard so much about.

Remy had made good on his promise.

The Steel Veins had finally arrived to settle a very old debt.

It wasn't long until I heard the gunshots over the roar of my bike's engine. The raid had started. Long years of karmic restitution were now rearing up to bite the Broken Veins in the ass.

When the feds wouldn't take care of the problem, I had to find someone who would. After a few extremely warily received phone calls, I was finally able to appeal directly to the Steel Veins' national president, Remy Daniels himself.

It turned out that they'd been looking for where the Broken Veins' annual was taking place since the club broke off. When I offered to give them live audio of my meeting with Ratchet in exchange for them coming in and making national news by wiping out most of their old rivals, Remy was understandably skeptical.

I laid out everything to him about my connection to the FBI, but he was thoroughly unmoved. It wasn't until I told him about Elisha's situation and how I was trying to help her that he even started to consider the offer. He didn't elaborate, but I got the feeling that he knew what it was like to give everything to save someone he cared about.

Of course, Remy would stage the assault in a way that his club couldn't be tied to it. When local authorities eventually showed up to investigate, it'd look like the gun cartel was the one to put the hit on the Broken Veins.

They'd chalk it up to a major gun deal that had gone very, very wrong.

Now all I had to do was see if it got big enough in the press to force the FBI to investigate. With the info I now had on this recorder, I was sure as hell useful, enough to negotiate a new deal that got me away from all this shit.

When I was far enough away, I pulled over and killed my engine. It felt damned good knowing I'd played a big part in bringing the hammer down on those malicious pricks. I almost wished I could've stuck around to see them get what they deserved.

The gunshots sounded like a fireworks display and continued for far too long.

Actually, I was glad I didn't see it. That was one bloodbath I could afford to miss.

As I was about to start the bike back up, my phone began to vibrate. It was Double D.

My stomach began to churn. With everything else going on, I'd forgotten all about him and the rest of my chapter. My heart sank at the realization. Of all the people to get killed or captured, those motherfuckers topped the list.

*They should've been at the farm.*

"Hey, Pres." I buried my concern and anger under layers of practiced dark casualness. "What's up?"

"Cowboy, Cowboy, Cowboy." The name leaked from Double D's lips like the steady drip of venom from a viper's fang. I felt the slightest crack run along my stone-cold biker facade. "Turns out you weren't completely honest with us, brother."

I stayed quiet. I had no idea how to respond. The cracks in my cover, my armor, deepened and spiderwebbed. My mind raced with the agonizing possibilities. Was I made? Did they somehow finally figure it out?

Then again, did it really matter if they had?

I didn't have to play pretend anymore.

It would be so damned easy to hang up and walk away, but something nagged at me to stay on the phone.

"For a guy who's good with a quick story or joke, you're awful quiet." His voice was thick with the superiority of certainty. Double D was a bulldog; once he got his teeth into a target, there was no prying them apart. If he wanted blood, which he so often did, he would get it.

A wide, sharp smile split my face. He had no idea what just happened to the rest of the club. While I reveled over exactly how I was going to give him the news, he continued.

"That's fine. We have a new storyteller now. Don't we?" He sneered. "Say hi, pumpkin."

*Pumpkin?* I didn't have to contemplate who he meant for long.

There was a whispered, defiant "No" in the background. A short, stubborn silence followed that was broken only by a slap, then finally a scream.

I knew instantly that it was Elisha. Any satisfaction I had building was immediately dashed.

The thought of not going after her never made it past my subconscious. It was just the opposite—I'd never been surer of anything in my entire life. The sun would rise, the moon would glow, and I would find her.

If that meant leaving a wake of bodies in my path, then so be it.

I'd spent hundreds of thousands of words over the course of two years building and maintaining my biker persona. It only took one to tear it all down.

"Where?" The word escaped me not as a question, but as a hard, unyielding demand.

I heard an amused laugh on the other end of the line. By owning up to it, or even caring about the owner of the scream, I'd basically admitted what he'd already assumed. Now they knew beyond doubt that I was the rat.

"The carnival at San Andino." The amusement drained from my former pres's voice. All that was left was a tone that promised nothing but violence. "Two hours. And don't bring any of your new federal friends with you."

That last part wouldn't be a problem. I doubted Harris would even answer my calls at the moment.

When Double D started oinking, I ended the call.

I scoffed, pulling up my recently dialed numbers. If Double D thought I wasn't bringing help to what was obviously a trap, he was out of his fucking mind.

If this just involved me, I might have gone and met them

alone, but this was Elisha who was in trouble. Egos aside, I wasn't going to take the chance.

Just before I made one last call, a terrible moment of hesitance struck me like a rock to the face.

Unless they were standing behind me, fuck 'em. The Broken Veins as an organization was being ripped to shreds right down the road. Double D and the rest of the chapter were nothing now. They were just some armed assholes who would be twisting in the wind without a support network. They had bigger problems than finding me now. Eventually they'd be forced into hiding from the Steel Veins wanting to clean them up.

And with no Broken Veins to inform on, I was *technically* free. At least until the FBI got around to giving a shit about me again.

Could I really throw everything away for a girl I'd literally just met, and whose last name I didn't even know?

The thought immediately made me feel nauseous.

So what if I didn't know her last name?

My whole life had been one compromise after another. I'd sold out my associates for the undercover deal just so I could sell out the Broken Veins to the FBI. All I'd ever done was keep myself alive, while never truly knowing why I should even bother. I drew breath strictly out of habit.

And sooner or later, I'd find a way to kick that habit too.

Elisha was just so damn different.

Going against the Broken Veins for any reason was insane, but she rose to face the insurmountable challenges head-on. It wasn't just because of the money; she did it to prove to herself that she could. Even in the face of death, she refused to back down and give up.

Elisha was incredible in so many ways, and she gave me hope that I could be a better version of myself. If I had even the faintest glimmer of a chance to save her, I had to take it.

To hell with the man I'd always been. It was time to be better than that.

*"It can be incredibly rewarding to do the right things for the right reasons."* Elisha's voice cooed in my mind, and I knew that this—that *she*—was worth fighting for.

I blew out my breath and dialed the number. Fuck the consequences.

Remy didn't answer, of course, so I left a message explaining the situation and what I needed. This was another in a long line of gambits. For all I knew, Remy could be lying facedown on that farm, drowning on his own blood. No one might ever hear my message for help. It was also the only number I had, so I had to take it on faith that he'd not only survive but also come save my sorry ass. He had no reason to—it wasn't part of our deal—but I swallowed my pride and begged anyway.

*You're not doing this for yourself,* I reminded myself. *It's for Elisha.*

I would go after her either way, but if I didn't have any help, it would be a token effort. It'd just be a way for Elisha and me to be killed together instead of being hunted down separately.

It was with her in mind that I stuffed my phone in my pocket and turned my bike on. I would rescue her and put the MC life behind me, or I'd die in the process. One way or another, this fake life I'd been living was over.

It felt amazing to have a worthwhile purpose again. She made me feel truly alive, and no force on earth could take that from me. Live or die, I would do so by her side. Funny, I'd always feared death, either at the hands of my club or in prison. Turned out what I was actually scared of wasn't dying—it was dying for nothing.

Elisha's pearly, slightly crooked smile roared in my heart and mind like a raging bonfire. If I had to die now, it would be for something. With a steely resolve and my gaze locked dead ahead, I wasn't afraid anymore.

I twisted the throttle, and the bike sped off like it was fired from a gun. I was now the bullet aimed at Double D and the rest of my chapter.

# Chapter 15
## ELISHA

My ribs ached the worst. I had clipped them at full force on a door handle when the bikers dragged me from the hotel room. The raw image of the cleaning lady's blood splattered all over the food clung to me as I clung to the crazy notion of escape.

I needed to get away.

It was a waste of energy. The Broken Veins took me easily.

Aside from the poor woman's murder, the worst part of the abduction was all the averted eyes from people we passed. *Bastards.*

Customers, staff, everyone was too afraid to help. They just looked at the floor when the four burly bikers dragged me out of there. No one raised a voice to stop something so obviously wrong.

The hotel Mason and I stayed in wasn't a cheap, sketchy motel. It wasn't the kind of place that had five deadbolts behind the door and bars over the windows. It wasn't super nice either, but it had multiple floors, a pool, an exercise room, and even a concierge booth.

When we'd checked in, the normalcy and familiarity of it all made me feel safe. It was a time-out from all the mayhem and danger. It was like I'd pressed Pause on an action film to go to the bathroom and grab some more popcorn. Kenneth and I stayed at these kinds of places whenever we vacationed or traveled for work.

I'd never even heard of something like this ever happening. And yet here I was, my eyes desperately scanning everyone, *anyone*, hoping just one person would meet my gaze. That just one person of the dozens we passed would be brave enough to cry out or threaten to call the cops.

Anything!

No one did.

Those scared, weak bastards were too paralyzed and thankful that it wasn't happening to them. I was sure someone called the police, but we were long gone before they arrived. And from the way these devils drove, I knew no one would be able to catch up to us.

I didn't even know what was going on until they eventually stopped by the side of the road and called Mason. When I heard his voice faintly through the phone, it made my heart somersault. I never thought I'd see or hear from him again.

Most of the conversation was Double D's taunts and verbal stabs. It was only when all eyes fell back on me that I realized what my role here truly was. I was the bait in their twisted game. The whole concept repulsed me.

I wanted nothing more than to call out to him, scream

his name. *Mason, please help me!* If I did, he would probably come.

That foolish hope burned like a coal furnace inside me. It was the same way my insides felt when he wrapped his arms around me. I was terrified of these men and what they would do. Care, concern, and safety were but words away; all I had to do was ask for them, and Mason would come.

How could I not cry out for him?

I immediately felt selfish and ashamed. His club knew the truth about him now. He would have to come alone and face off against four vicious criminals. How could even he survive that?

I narrowed my eyes. Breathing out, I shook my head. I refused to play their game.

I wouldn't call out for him if that meant watching him die. I couldn't bear that burden. I knew they were going to kill me regardless of if he showed up or not. As scared as I was, it was better to die cold and alone knowing I wasn't responsible for his death too.

This whole thing was my fault, after all. If I'd just let him go before we got to Carver, all of this would've been avoided. I didn't know if it was pride or stubbornness, but I'd had a chance to walk away, and I didn't take it.

With a look from his pres, Ginge, the bearded, red-haired monster, tested my high ideals with a backhand. My lip split under the force of the blow. I held my breath, fighting back a whimper. I remained firm until the cherry tip of a cigarette surprised the side of my neck.

My own body betrayed me. I screamed, then slumped low.

"Where?" Mason's voice boomed like a thunder strike through the phone's receiver.

I should've rejoiced in knowing that he intended to come for me. Who wouldn't jump at the thought of rescue? But it only made my heart all the heavier. With that one act of weakness, I'd just signed his death warrant.

I'd failed him.

It was another long ride before we pulled into the derelict carnival at San Andino. Between despair and resignation, my head filled with curiosity. What could a carnival down here look like? I speculated that it might resemble some I'd been to when I was a child. Maybe there were people here who could help me.

I couldn't have been more wrong.

When the bike engines were all silenced, there was a moment of deathly calm. No one spoke; they just gazed at the carnival. The only sounds on the horizon were of the howling wind whipping over rusted metal and the groan of great wooden structures as they slightly swayed with dogged consistency.

I'd stepped from one twisted reality into another. The decaying bones of a long-since-abandoned amusement park haunted a small stretch of landscape that over decades was being reclaimed by nature.

It was a chilling sight.

We couldn't possibly be headed *in* there, could we? The danger of the situation was overtaken by a deep unsettling in my nerves. The hair on my arms stood on end. That was where Mason and I would die?

If there were ever a portal to Hell on this earth, I imagined it would look a lot like this.

"Spaz, stay here," Double D barked. "Let us know when you hear movement."

The Broken Veins' pres was as unfazed as if he were stepping into the convenience store for snacks. If this sight was normal to them. How many other people had they dragged here?

"The fuck do I have to stay for?" Spaz protested. He was considerably more fazed.

"Don't be such a bitch." Ginge flexed one massive arm and shoved Spaz with ease. It sent the scruffy rail of a man nearly toppling over. "It's not haunted, you fucking pussy. Besides, with Cowboy out, you're the new blood again."

"Fuck you, you troll-looking motherfucker!" Spaz shot back, his hand sinking to his pistol.

Maybe they would kill each other and I could escape in the darkness and confusion.

That dream only lasted a few steps before someone's greasy hand wrapped around my arm and wrenched me backward.

"Enough fucking around. When you hear Cowboy's bike, give a call, then come meet us. Everyone else, let's go," Double D growled. He dragged me into the park, under a weather-worn arch that, in faded, once-red letters, said 'Welcome to Fantasy Zone!'

My head swam and my throat tightened with each new horror that was unveiled in the beams of the Broken Veins' flashlights. Large plastic clown heads that wept paint and grime hung over near-collapsed game booths. Hideous dead-eyed faces smiled dumbly back at us at every turn.

Age, weather, and neglect had taken what was once probably innocent and cheesy and made it into the stuff of nightmares. At any moment I felt that something would come alive and swallow me whole.

I looked up at the moon for a sense of something familiar, something I could understand. Soon that too was broken by the few stubborn sections of a skeletal roller coaster that seemed to defy gravity. Its silhouette was easily the tallest thing in the park. It stood like a gravestone over a plot of rainbow-colored death.

My chest and throat became coarse, and a new worry began to strangle me. An asthma worry. I hadn't been able to bring my inhaler. If I had an attack right now, I might not survive long enough to even see Mason. Tears welled in my eyes at the grim thought.

"Where are you, Mason?" I said too softly for the bikers to hear. A gentle breeze almost stole the sound from my own ears. I needed to hear his name spoken aloud for it to feel real. The sandpaper in my throat subsided just a little at the comfort in his name. "Mason," I whispered again.

We passed a carousel, an arcade station, and even a walled-in bumper cars ring before finally coming to a stop at the teacup ride. I was shoved into one of the filthy cups, unceremoniously landing on leaves and other dried *matter.* The back shell of the cup had large rotted-through holes in it. The thought of groping hands coming in from the pitch-blackness behind me was horrifying.

One of the bikers lifted a crate from another teacup. What they pulled out of it finally made me understand why we came here. Each man tucked away his pistol and grabbed an assault rifle. It looked like they were preparing for war, or a slaughter.

I felt even worse now about that scream earlier. How could Mason possibly hope to survive this? I prayed he wouldn't come after me.

Double D frowned at his watch.

Ginge decided to check on the biker they'd left behind. "Anything yet, fuckface?" he asked into his phone. A brief conversation later, Ginge shook his head at his pres and closed the phone. Growing frustrated, the fiery red-haired troll turned to me.

"Where the fuck is your rat boyfriend, bitch?" He kicked my teacup for added punctuation.

I jolted backward from the force of the blow, rusted metal crumbling down onto me in small sheets. Three sets of angry eyes fell on me, demanding answers.

I'd never felt so small.

A gunshot in the distance mercifully drew everyone's attention away from me. It got me worried though, especially when one shot became four or five.

*Was that Mason?*

The crushing thought of him not being all right ruined me. I scanned for any way I could possibly help him. I had to do something.

The only thing I saw that I might be able to reach was Double D's knife. It was in a sideways holster along the back of his belt. While they were distracted calling Spaz and scanning the dark landscape, I was slowly inching toward the knife handle.

"No answer. Weaselly fuck had one job." Ginge looked gravely at his pres, who idly stepped just out of my reach. I jerked my arm away at the last second to avoid detection.

My breathing came in a torrent. What was I thinking? I didn't have any kind of plan after I got the knife. There were still three of them with *guns*. What the hell was I going to do with a measly knife?

The third biker, whose name I hadn't even learned, walked a dozen steps away and peered around the corner of some kind of ticket booth. He was flashing his light back toward the entrance, hoping to see some signs of movement. After a minute or so, he turned back to the group. "I don't see anything. Should we go back for—"

A gunshot split the air, cutting the man off. I didn't see where the biker was hit. All I saw was his flashlight flip out of his hand and smash against the ground, momentarily dimming with the impact.

He was highlighted a second later by the remaining two Broken Veins. The bullet had caught him in the jaw and blew open his throat. He was writhing from the pain, clutching the wound uselessly.

I had to turn away from the gore and the gurgling of the dying man. The only solace in my heart was that I knew he deserved it. They all did.

"Skip!" Ginge cried out, setting off after his friend. Double D took aim over Ginge's shoulder and shot the dying man in the head, dropping him instantly. "Fuck!" Ginge and I recoiled from the noise and the suddenness.

I didn't know why he did it. Maybe the pres knew the man was a lost cause and was putting him out of his misery, or maybe he didn't want the wounded man blocking any of his shots.

When that last muzzle flash lit Double D's face, it showed only a cold indifference in putting the man down. He gave it the same amount of emotion and concern as someone ordering a coffee.

How could anyone hope to stop a man like him?

Both of the remaining Broken Veins unloaded their assault rifles in wide sweeps, having no clear idea where the shot came from. Their muzzle flashes lit them with rapid strobes of light.

"Here, piggy, piggy, piggy!" The pres turned to the darkness and hollered, "I know you're out there, Cowboy! You got ten seconds to step into the light, or I start taking pieces off your girl here!"

Double D pulled his knife and put the blade just beneath my ear. I screamed. I couldn't help it. Smiling, he breathed in my pain and terror, *then* started counting. He started at five and counted up from there. My head and neck stretched upward, trying to escape the pressure of the sharp knife.

One jerk and I would be disfigured for the rest of my short life.

"I'm here" came the voice I both prayed for and dreaded to hear at the same time. Mason had arrived, and I'd led him right into a trap.

It was painful, but also wonderful. He didn't have to come, and I wasn't sure he even would. I had so many doubts when he left earlier today, but now I knew. My insides glowed like a lit pumpkin. I felt whole and full.

Mason did care about me!

"Don't worry. You won't have to watch us kill your boyfriend," Double D whispered into my knife-held ear. The sadistic biker gently stroked the flyaway strands of hair from my forehead. "I'll kill you first."

I wish I could've said that I spat in his face and swore at him. If it were anyone else, I might have done just that, but this man shook me to the core. Everything from his presence and his grin to the sudden volcanic fluctuations in his eyes was cruel and unpredictable. The Broken Veins' pres was the kind of in-control crazy that would drown puppies in a pond while casually feeding the ducks bits of bread.

I fought hard to keep my fear from tipping into a downward spiral. A potential stress-induced asthma attack hung over me like imminent rain from dark, crackling storm clouds.

*Breathe, Elisha! Control it!*

My grasp on that control wavered a bit when Double D slid the knife away. He made a small, painful slice where the skin on my neck met my ear.

Blood trickled between my fingers as I put pressure on the wound. I stifled a cry of pain; I wouldn't give him the satisfaction. That much I could still manage.

"Step into the light, pig." Pres replaced his knife and brought up his rifle.

A man-shaped sliver of darkness broke away from the inky black of deep shadow. The crunching of gravel beneath Mason's boots alerted the bikers to his location, and just as quickly, they bathed him with their flashlights.

Mason wore no leather vest, just the black T-shirt from earlier and a pair of dirty jeans. Long lines of blood had run up and then back down his forearms, starting and ending at his glossy red hands. His face and neck were spattered with blotches as well. From the way he walked, confident, strong, and without fear, I knew none of the blood was his.

I shuddered to think of what he'd done to the biker who was left behind. Ginge shook his head at the sight, making peace with the fact that Spaz was dead.

I thought of the poor maid and what they'd done to her, and an angry part of me was glad at the brutal image of Mason. I hoped he'd made that sadistic bastard suffer for what he'd done.

Mason tossed his pistol, knowing it would be the next demand. He raised his arms slightly to show he had no other weapons. If he was afraid of the firing squad that now stood in front of him, you'd never know it to look at him.

His raw defiance at certain death gave me goose bumps. My heart skipped when I first saw him, but now it just raced. I was staring at an avenging angel.

He had to have a plan, right? He must have. It was suicide otherwise.

"I had such hopes for you, Cowboy." The pres fired off a round past Mason; it sparked off something metal in the distance. I gasped, feeling a rush of blood through my heart.

Mason closed his eyes and cocked his head but otherwise remained unflinching.

"I was going to make you vice!" Double D fired another shot, a tuft of dirt erupting near Mason's boots. "It breaks my heart to know you're the fucking rat."

"Well, you know what they say about sinking ships and rats." Mason shrugged.

"The fuck are you talking about?" Ginge barked.

"I take it you haven't talked to anyone at the annual recently, then?" Mason asked.

Double D's eyes narrowed.

"You missed a hell of a fireworks display." Mason smirked. "Steel Veins raided the farm. I hear it was a bloody mess."

"Bullshit." Ginge searched his pres for any kind of input. He received a nod, not of confirmation but one that told him to look into it.

Ginge spent the next several long minutes calling members who were at the annual. Finally, hanging up one last time, he shook his head.

"How long, you traitorous piece of shit? Were you working us the whole time?"

"You really want to know?" Mason cocked his head slightly. "Hell, I'll tell you everything. It's not like it matters now anyway. But first you're going to tell me how you found us in North Carolina."

"The same way we found her at the hotel in Memphis." Double D abruptly laughed, as if it was all a joke. And maybe it *was* a joke to him. Who could know what happened in that twisted evil brain of his. "Your girlfriend's real boyfriend."

"Kenneth? How?" I barely registered the words as they slunk out of my lips.

I was dazed with the revelation. That was all wrong. My ex-fiancé didn't fit in anywhere in this dark world of death and intrigue. He was pissed that I wouldn't return his calls, but he wouldn't want to see me dead.

Would he?

No. He was a lot of things—a cheater, a coward, a terrible partner and lover—but not that.

"We ran her plates when you two ran off together. Once we found out who she was and where she worked, getting to him was nothing," Ginge growled. "Only took a few minutes before he told us everything. The hotel she was at, your rap sheet, the bounty, fucking everything. We barely even had to threaten him."

"You called him?" Mason turned to me. I didn't know what felt worse, the accusation in Mason's voice or the look of betrayal in his eyes. Both cut me to the bone. If I was going to die, I wanted it to be right then.

"No! I swear." And I hadn't. All I'd done was turn my phone on and check…. The synapses in my brain fired like a lightning strike. In a flash, I knew exactly what happened. "The GPS on my phone."

He must have turned it on remotely. He knew where I was the whole time.

For the first time since all of this started, I felt my blood boil. My face twisted in rage. *That fucking asshole! He'd tell a gang of murderous bikers where I was before he told the police or came himself?*

I was too angry to notice my chest rising and falling in rapid succession. My speeding pulse thrummed in my ears. I was too pained to feel the tightening in my lungs and my airways swelling. I just thought it was all part of my own feelings of betrayal.

Mason began to speak, but my cough cut him off.

It was only when I saw all the warm, tawny color in his face drain to ashen gray that I realized with horror that an asthma attack was coming on. One of my hands drifted to my throat, but without my inhaler, there was no stopping it.

I was going to drown in a sea of oxygen. Not even Mason could save me from myself.

For the first time, I saw real fear on his face. He was about to lose something far more important than his own life. Even if he saved me, he was going to lose me.

We'd both just run out of time.

Everyone knew the time for talk was over. It was now time to get down to the bloody business.

Mason darted forward with the reckless abandon of someone who was bulletproof. I lunged for the pres, but even if I could distract him, Ginge was too far away for me to stop.

*Oh God, I'm going to watch the man I love die.*

*Love?*

The word crashed into me as I crashed into Double D. I grabbed the handle of what I hoped was his gun. We thrashed together for a moment before he threw me back into the teacup. I collapsed into a fit of coughing and began to feel light-headed. I didn't have his gun, just his knife.

*I love Mason? When did that happen?*

But how could I not? It was the only thing that felt right in all this madness. I did love him.

I watched Mason close the distance between him and Ginge. Why hadn't the burly redhead opened fire on Mason, killing him on the spot? A silly part of me thought that maybe Mason was bulletproof, that maybe he couldn't be killed and he actually had a chance. It was completely insane, but I needed something to keep me going.

Then I saw the red dot.

Immediately I understood why, instead of firing, Ginge had raised his arms. Mason had been stalling. All the talk and questions weren't for his benefit but for the snipers to get into position. That was his plan.

*Oh God. He must have told his FBI handler about me and about what happened!* That would be the only way he could get snipers out to a carnival in the middle of the night. How much trouble was he in now?

How much of his freedom did he have to throw away just to save me?

But I quickly realized it wasn't a sniper or the FBI that was the source of the red dot.

A man appeared from the inky blackness holding a semiautomatic rifle. He was white and had shaggy, midlength, rusty brown hair, dark eyes, and a light beard. The black vest he wore over his armor had the white patch of the Steel Veins, and beneath that was another patch that said 'National Pres.'

Ginge's head exploded.

This new man's eyes were the coldest things I'd ever seen, sending shivers up my spine. Whoever he was, violence was as much a part of him as my limbs were to me. He looked like something out of a horror movie.

Where did Mason find this guy?

"Your boyfriend is cheating" came Double D's voice somewhere behind me. A renewed sense of dread filled me. He was using me as a shield.

Mason darted past Ginge's corpse, snatching the pistol at his waist. I screamed his name in warning, but only labored wheezes came out. Wheezes that were quickly drowned out by more gunfire. Mason dodged as best he could, but not even he could outrun a bullet.

His body jerked from the impact and doubled over.

*No!* He couldn't be dead. I refused to accept that. I reached out to Mason but was stopped by the gnarled hands of the Broken Veins' president.

Double D had reached through the backside of the teacup's rotting metal shell, and with a mighty heave, he pulled me right through it. When I hit the ground, I looked up and saw there was no red dot on him.

No one had this monster in their sights.

I felt powerless, broken. My will to resist drained away.

"Elisha!" Mason called out to me from somewhere. A wave of relief washed over me even as I was dragged off into the dark hellscape.

*He's alive.*

Double D had me by my hair, dragging and wrenching.

I couldn't stand up or get my bearings, and I was coughing so hard now that I could barely see. It felt like I was perpetually falling, inside and out. My chest burned from all the wheezing.

Even though Mason was alive, he was so far away. He'd never get to me before Double D realized he could go much faster if he didn't have a hostage. It was hard to maintain any kind of hope, especially when things seemed so desperate. If I weren't in the throes of the worst asthma attack I'd ever had, I might've been able to figure some way out of this....

*"Self-pity is a broken crutch."* My father's words rang through me.

I didn't need hope or eyes or self-pity, I decided. I needed to stop making excuses, and I needed to slow this bastard down.

My knuckles tightened around the knife I'd pulled from the biker when I lunged for him earlier. I caught my footing just long enough to turn and slice wildly. I wasn't aiming for anything specifically. It was too dark and chaotic for aim.

I just wanted to hurt him.

What happened next was like a pressure valve releasing all at once and with explosive force. The blade sank hungrily into the back of his knee. He released me immediately. There was a lull where he gasped in air to scream and then a loud snap, like an elastic band retracting.

In the chasing flashlights behind us, I saw what I'd done. Double D's severed hamstring shot up into his ass with such force that it bowled him headlong. He screamed and whined with pain as I rolled away.

The lack of oxygen forced my sight to go black, only occasional strobes of vision filtering through. I saw Mason catch up. He was bleeding a lot, but that didn't seem to slow him down. I heard more gunfire.

My breathing was down to a pinhole. I couldn't concentrate on anything for more than a second at a time. In my last few flashes of vision, I saw Mason kick his old president's gun from his hand, then bring his heavy boot down on the man's head.

Then the air refused to come at all. I couldn't breathe.

"Elisha!" Mason's scream was so distant now even though he was close physically. I felt him lift me off the ground. Who knew where he was taking me? I no longer had the ability to ask.

It was funny. All this danger that orbited around us, and the thing that would truly be our undoing was something I carried within me the whole time. Damn asthma.

What a mundane way to die.

"You need to hang on." Mason sounded like the whisper of a dream. My cold, numb lips felt the exhalation of his breath. Air that my useless lungs couldn't draw in. "I'm getting you help."

Mason yelled to someone else who I couldn't see. There was a lot of commotion and flashing lights around me.

"You're not allowed to die!" Little wet drops fell from him and speckled my cheeks.

Was Mason crying for me?

Was I already dead?

Just before I blacked out for the last time, Mason said a few last words. "I love y—"

# Epilogue
## MASON

The cabbie half turned over his shoulder and asked, "This the place?"

My grandmother's blue house with white trim grew larger as he drove us up to it.

"Yeah."

I snorted at the irony of it all. Of course I'd be back here. Whenever I fucked up during my childhood, I'd always been sent away to my grandmother's house. I felt like a little kid again.

I walked to the front door, letting the full weight of these past five months sink in.

After the news of what happened on the farm broke to national coverage as the biggest gangland slaughter in history, second only to the Steel Veins' coup a few years earlier, the public's attention was firmly back on the war against biker violence. That also meant the FBI needed to respond publicly to the threat.

Harris and company picked me up within twenty-four hours of the news breaking, eager to continue our working relationship. I stopped them immediately. I told them if they wanted the evidence I had from the meeting with Ratchet, then they were going to have to write up a new deal this time.

It was a deal I had personally written and had a team of lawyers go over.

With heavy reluctance, Harris finally agreed to my demands, and I agreed to cooperate.

For five long months, I was sequestered away in a protective services compound while the FBI pored over every file I'd ever sent them. They cataloged all the evidence I'd collected over the last few years to put a case together against Ratchet's distribution network.

I had logged an extensive amount of files on the Broken Veins and had incriminating evidence on members of almost every chapter. All the horrible things they did were coming to light. I'd collected enough to put the surviving members of my own chapter away for a couple of lifetimes.

Of course, not everyone from the Broken Veins was at the farm during the raid, but that didn't matter. Between the FBI working diligently to bring them down and the Steel Veins looking to finish the job on the renegade organization, things weren't looking good for whoever was left in the Broken Veins.

It was very rewarding to see the wicked brought to justice, but it was even better to be the one responsible for it. I felt kind of… vindicated, like I had been able to wash away some of my own grime in the process. For the first time in my life, I was on the side of the angels.

It felt good.

The FBI wasn't fully convinced of my good intentions.

The other reason they held me for so damn long was to make sure I hadn't committed any criminal activities of my own while undercover. That part had me nervous. I had always been extremely careful, but running with a crew as bad as the Broken Veins meant getting my hands dirty every now and then just to avoid suspicion.

It was never anything serious, some breaking and entering, threatening people, and starting fights mostly. But this was the FBI, and I was a criminal; if they could put me away, they would.

After an agonizingly long investigation and interrogation, it was Harris himself who told me I was clean and that the FBI had no further use for me, "so stay out of trouble."

I'd come to find out that Harris had interrogated Elisha as well, but she was very used to dealing with cops of all types. She told them only what they wanted to hear and left out anything that might be used against us. As far as they knew, she'd had her car stolen, then was kidnapped from her hotel in Memphis. She told them it was a random act of violence. She had no idea what happened to the biker gang after she slipped away when they weren't paying attention.

Officially, Ginge, Skip, Spaz, and Double D were fugitives on the run, but I knew we wouldn't have to worry about them anymore. Remy made sure they'd never be found. The FBI would never know about the carnival, my brief alliance with Remy and the Steel Veins, or Elisha's rescue.

The rescue. That was the worst part. My chest tightened at the memory.

Elisha had stopped breathing by the time I got her to a nearby hospital. She went without oxygen for three and a half agonizing minutes. I fell apart when the doctors made me leave her. I had to wait in another room while they tried to bring her back from the dead.

Standing there not being able to help in any way was the worst moment of my life.

It wasn't long after I found out she was all right that the FBI picked me up. They wouldn't let me into her room to comfort her.

Bastards.

Over the next five months I wasn't allowed to see her. They only let me call her a few times, and everything we said to each other was recorded and analyzed.

I didn't give a shit, though. It was just so good to hear her voice. The things I told her I was going to do to her when they let me go were sure to make anyone listening blush. Knowing she was all right was the only thing that kept me sane through the whole process. Each call just made me miss her so much more.

Walking through the empty familiar rooms of my grandma's house gave me a sense of warm nostalgia. There were no video games here, and I never had any friends to play with nearby. I chuckled that my parents thought of this place as a punishment for me when in reality I always loved it here.

Sure, it was stuffy and everything was old, but my

grandma filled the place with a sense of welcoming and warmth that I'd never found back at home.

I guess that would explain why I came back here so often, even when I was well into my twenties. Whenever I screwed up so bad that I had to lie low, I would just escape back here and forget about things for a while. She was always there when I needed her.

It always haunted me that I never returned the favor.

When she fell ill, I was too busy building my criminal empire to be where I should've been. Looking back, my important reasons for staying away were just flimsy excuses. I'd call her and wish her well, but I never came to visit. I was too scared to see her like that. I had trouble wrapping my head around how such a wonderful woman could be brought so low.

When she passed away, she took all the house's warmth and love with her. I was surprised to hear that had she left the place to me in her will. The only time I ever came back was to lick my wounds or to tinker with shit in the garage.

My fondest childhood memory was now just a monument to my shame.

Walking in this time felt different. Somehow the house wasn't as depressing as it was just a few months ago when I brought Elisha here. I looked around a bit more, but nothing was physically out of place. It just *felt* different, in a good way.

I pushed open the garage door, expecting it to also be untouched; however, this time I was wrong. Someone had definitely been in here since I was away.

A new black-and-chrome motorcycle was parked in the middle of the messy workshop. I could see from the top of the stairs that it had a red bow and a small card attached to the handlebars.

A broad smile spread across my lips. Elisha had been here.

I dropped my bag and made my way over to it. While I was in protective custody, I told her that one of the first things they did was confiscate the bike I was riding. I never imagined she would do this.

It wasn't just that it was a gorgeous bike that made it so special. It was what the bike meant. The only thing I missed from my time with the Broken Veins was the riding. It got into my soul and carved out a little pocket that could never be filled with anything else.

I slid my hand over the black leather seats and onto the cool chrome gas tank. When I thought of freedom, I thought about riding a bike and not having to look into my rearview mirror.

And when I thought of happiness, I thought about Elisha's arms around my waist as I rode.

The card didn't say anything on the outside, and for a moment I thought, *What if this was all a mistake? Or some kind of threat?* My brow furrowed, but I shook the ridiculous notion from my head. I never told anyone in the club about this place, and if they had found it, I doubt they'd have left me a present.

I paused, then looked the bike over very carefully for bombs just in case. There were very few people left alive who knew about my role as an informant, but it always paid to be cautious. The bike was clean, my enemies were gone, and I was just being overly paranoid.

Finally opening the card, I was greeted with a picture. It was taped facedown with a note from Elisha scribbled on it. It read 'Bounty hunting company (under new management!) is actively seeking a ruggedly handsome criminal for an exciting new opportunity....'

I pulled the tape off the picture and turned it over.

"No shit." I smiled so wide that I thought my face was going to break in half.

I was staring at the ultrasound of my new son or daughter!

How the fuck did she keep this a secret from me for so long? I wasn't upset, I was amazed. I immediately wanted to tell everyone, but I had to settle for screaming it in the garage.

"I'm going to be a father! You hear that, Grandma? I'm going to be a dad!"

I had to lean against the bike to get my bearings. I'd never thought about being a parent, figuring I'd be dead before I ever had the chance. The feeling was incredible. There were so many things I could teach the kid, what to do and, more importantly, what *not* to do.

*Holy fuck, I might actually be good at this!*

Looking at the picture, I realized it wasn't the house that was less depressing, it was me. *I* had changed. The man I was could've never brought something that beautiful into the world. That version of me could never have deserved a woman like Elisha.

Tucking the picture of my son or daughter into my breast pocket, I started up my new bike. I had been gone far too long already and couldn't bear to be away for a second longer. I took one last look at the house and rode off to find the love of my life.

I would come back here again one day and clean the house out. Maybe I could even bring back some of the warmth I remembered so fondly from growing up, but that'd only be possible if my new family was with me.

"My new family." I liked the sound of that.

******

I parked my bike in front of the building. I'd never been to Elisha's office before, but I was looking forward to it. All the time I'd known her had been spent in my crazy world. It'd be interesting to see what her crazy world looked like for a change.

There was an argument booming through the building's stairwell as I entered it. I recognized the man's familiar baritone voice right away. The stream of curses was coming from Kenneth, Elisha's ex, the one who'd sold her out to the Broken Veins. He was a few floors above me and on his way down.

I couldn't wait to meet him in person.

I saw him first when he rounded the corner that put him on my landing. He was too caught up in yelling and gesturing at Elisha to notice me. He was carrying an empty printer paper box full of his belongings. A few framed photos flopped over and crashed against the steps when he walked into me.

Kenneth was flustered, his collared shirt untucked from his black slacks and his nice vest wrinkled and askew. About my height but fifty pounds leaner, he bounced off me like a bird off a window. His dark brown face was red tinged with angry indignation that I was blocking his path.

"Hey! Get the hell out of my—" He began to turn his tirade on me, but I cut him off.

"My name's Mason," I calmly replied. "Elisha may have mentioned me."

"Oh… shit." Kenneth's eyes flared. He tried to push past me and flee down the staircase.

I grabbed a fistful of his vest and shoved him backward. The box with his assorted items slipped from his hands and sent the contents clattering down the stairwell. I pushed him up against the wall. "What's the rush, Ken?"

"Hey, I-I don't want any trouble."

"Is that what you told the Broken Veins when they called you?"

"I didn't have a choice!" Kenneth's face fell. "They knew everything about me. They were going to come to my house, man. My home. Where I sleep!"

"The big bad bikers forced you to, huh?" I narrowed my eyes at him. Kenneth looked down slightly but didn't answer. "You don't have to worry about them anymore. They're all in jail now. Well, not all of them. I did have to kill a few."

Kenneth's eyes flashed again at my last remark.

"I didn't know what they were gonna do. I had no choice—"

"Stop," I demanded. I'd known the man a few minutes and was already tired of his bullshit. How the hell did Elisha tolerate him for so many years?

"You didn't know what the vicious motorcycle club was going to do to your ex-fiancée when they caught up to her?" My question dripped with incredulity. "Grow a fucking backbone, you prick."

He frowned but kept his mouth shut.

"Now, because you're so good at following orders." My eyes twitched from holding back the urge to cave his skull in for putting Elisha in so much danger. She was lucky to be alive. "Here's what happens next. You're going to leave here and never bother Elisha again."

"There's nothing I'd love more." He grimaced. "But she and the courts have other plans, apparently."

I thought about pressing him further, but I released him instead. I'd heard that his involvement was flagged by the FBI. That couldn't look good for his stake in any business disputes between him and Elisha. Maybe that was why he was the one to clean out his desk and not her.

"Can I go?" He asked it like a timid child might request to go to the bathroom during class.

I said nothing but released him roughly.

Kenneth refused to meet my gaze, looking especially defeated as he scuttled down the stairs. He left all his scattered belongings except for an old high school sports trophy.

"Kenny," I called back to him when he stopped to pick up the trophy. He looked up at me with cautious resignation.

"If Elisha tells me that you're being an asshole, I will come for you."

The dread sparkling in his eyes was all the confirmation I needed.

I didn't wait for any kind of reply, just put the whole thing out of my mind and walked up the last few flights that would bring me home. I pushed open the third-floor door to their offices.

Elisha was facing away from me, gleefully cleaning out the receptionist's desk right into the trash. Looked like Chelsea was going to need a new job too.

I leaned silently against the doorframe, admiring Elisha. She was wearing a dress. It was a modest knee-length blue number, but it was a dress nevertheless. Her hair wasn't in a bun either. It was thick, curly, and confidently hanging down past her shoulders.

With the bump of her stomach pushing out the blue fabric of her dress, she was even prettier than I remembered.

Elisha whirled at the door closing behind me, probably expecting to resume the fight with Kenneth. Instead, she saw me and her face lit up.

"Hi," she said. Her breathing was quickened, most likely from the messy argument, but it was calming at about the same rate it took the slow smile to creep across her face. Her eyes turned up and became glossy.

"I didn't know if you'd…."

*She didn't know if I'd come back.* I could read that in the relief on her features. *She thought the picture of the baby scared me off?*

I walked over and brushed the hair out of her face. I looked hard into her eyes. "How could I not?"

"We barely knew each other then." Elisha looked down and rubbed her stomach. "A lot can change in almost half a year." She regarded me with worried eyes again.

I smiled and bent low, then placed a hand on her stomach. "I can see that. Boy or girl?"

"She's a girl," she said softly.

I kissed her stomach and then laughed. I couldn't contain my excitement any longer. Elisha squealed as I carefully picked her up. Her hair cascaded down to tickle the sides of my head. Beaming smiles adorned both our faces.

"I've missed you so goddamn much," I said, gazing deeply into her eyes.

Now it was her turn to laugh. Tears of joy trailed down her full cheeks as I kissed her. It was a kiss five months overdue. And one I hadn't been able to stop thinking about the whole time I was gone.

I gently placed her back onto the floor. "So, a dress, huh? I didn't think you had it in you."

"It just felt… right, somehow." She bit the corner of her bottom lip. Her life had changed dramatically since meeting me. She could've either let her fear reject those changes or be strong enough to embrace them. I was glad to see she was still strong enough for the latter.

"It's no cowboy hat, but it'll do." Elisha snorted at that but smiled regardless. I continued, "About this job. Are you sure you want another boyfriend as a business partner?"

"Partner?" Elisha scoffed, then pushed a finger into my

chest playfully. "You're an ex-con. You'll be working *for* me, not with me."

"Sure thing, Warden." I feigned a quick salute and pulled her in to me for another hug.

"Are we crazy?" she asked after a long while.

These last few months without her were unbearable. It felt like I was wandering a desert, on the cusp of dying from dehydration. Finally seeing Elisha was the cool cup of water I needed to survive.

"You're goddamn right we are." I kissed her again. "And I wouldn't have it any other way.

Home to me wasn't a building or a city, it was a feeling. Home was the crushing embrace of warm arms that I never thought I'd feel again. An embrace I knew I could never live without. She showed me the man I could be and made me feel whole.

I looked forward to spending the rest of my life returning the favor.

# The End

# Epilogue Two – Bonus Chapter
## MASON

"Are you sure?" she asked, biting the corner of her lip ever so lightly.

I nodded, knowing how much she wanted to try it. I clicked the handcuff closed around my wrist. What the hell? All things considered this was tame in the face of everything else we'd been through together.

"Okay." The uncertainty in her face burned away like fog at sunrise. She started toward me again, then stopped. Elisha slid her gun out of her holster, then placed it on the floor, safely away from the chained criminal. She looked at me with lusty eyes and exhaled, smiling. "The cuffs stay on," she said with authority, climbing onto my lap.

"I wouldn't have it any other way." I looped my free hand behind her back and pulled her stomach against mine.

Her breath, warm, sweet, and rapid, tickled my chin as we touched foreheads. I could feel her pulse in her fingertips. Excitement washed over me. Her nervousness made me smile. Elisha was so strong in many ways, but roleplaying like this brought out a vulnerability in her that she'd never show to anyone else.

I knew when I first saw her so long ago now that there was something special about her. Of course she was beautiful, but what really kept her in my thoughts was everything that surrounded that beauty. Her drive, her cunning, her intelligence and charm. She had also become an incredible mother to our beautiful, little girl.

I closed my eyes and focused on her scent, how she felt, the sound of her voice, and what she tasted like. I was in no rush. Elisha's best friend Star was watching our daughter, Ella, till tomorrow. Elisha and I rented a room in the shittiest motel we could find, and I wanted this night to last as long as possible. And I couldn't think of a better way to spend my time than with her.

I caught trace whiffs of her creamy lotion and the baking soda deodorant she wore. Her natural scent wasn't something I could describe with words. It was more of a feeling, maybe even a memory. Something sunny and warm and free.

Whatever it was, it made all the tension and stress I carried with me drain away. The rest of the trappings in my life now that I had joined the Steel Veins had become less important. I was fully in the moment with her. The full weight of her slight frame settled on my lap, and she draped her arms around my shoulders as we kissed.

I could taste lingering notes of spearmint on her lips. With each press, they slowly parted, allowing our teeth to briefly click together. Our tongues trespassed after that, sliding over each other with the tentative embrace that only young lovers knew. Her timidity gave way to lust before being overtaken by yearning.

My hand strained against the cutting metal shackle. With her just out of reach, I pulled all the harder. The pain only enhanced the desire to brush my fingers against the warmth of her thigh. Hearing the pipe flex, she spread her legs toward my clutching fingers. I greedily consumed every floating inch until finally grazing the slightly rough fabric of her pants.

My other hand had dipped beneath the hem of her shirt to explore the smooth nook in the small of her back. Her spine straightened with anticipation.

Smoldering embers within her began to catch. She drew long lines down my back with her fingertips and finished by curling her nails. The sting of it pushed me even farther into her.

Elisha hooked the bottom of my shirt and pulled it over my head. It slid down my arm to lie uselessly over my bound wrist and her thigh.

She kissed me while clumsily attempting to undo her shirt. I grasped between the gaps of several buttons and wrenched it to the sides. The buttons flew off in every direction like popcorn. She yelped, her mouth hanging open in surprise, yet her eyes narrowed in excitement. 'More of that,' they screamed at me.

Elisha had a bit of a devilish side to her that I'd never have pegged her for when we first met, especially given the professional way she'd always carried herself. The girl had some kink to her and I loved every second of it.

I reached beneath her ruined shirt, lightly grazed across her pink bra, and then cupped her breast hard. The corner of my mouth rose.

"Off," I demanded.

The hesitance within her surged only briefly before it was saturated by curiosity and lust. Embracing it, Elisha smiled wolfishly. In one grand movement, she pulled the whole mess of clothing, bra and all, over her head and tossed it to the floor. The light played off the cool tones in her radiant brown skin. I couldn't help but bask in her bare glow.

She was perfect.

Nothing I had previously been used to. All the hookups I'd found myself in, especially after joining the Broken Veins, were disposable. Girls who were passed around by the club with no attachment to anything but the drugs and the lifestyle. Even on my best days, I'd never been with someone who thrilled me as much as Elisha.

My brain felt flooded with sensation, and I moved by impulse. My tongue traced the grooves up the side of her stomach, over her ribs, and then up between her breasts. No one had ever tasted sweeter. Elisha let her head loll backward and dragged her nails over my scalp.

I kissed and nipped at her, raking my teeth over her tiny dark circles to skim past her hard nipples. I passed again. Each time, she'd arch a little closer. I wrapped my lips around her nipple, then my teeth, and sucked. My free fingers pinched and pulled at her other sepia nub.

Elisha ran her hand down my chest and began to rock her hips against mine. Through the many layers of thick fabric,

I felt her heat and pressure as she ground up the length of my stiff cock. The harder she pushed into me, the harder I bit down on her. She made me ache for more.

She popped the top button of my jeans, though I was hard enough to nearly do it myself. I couldn't stand it anymore. I could no longer be a passenger; I needed all of her. With one arm, I pressed her tightly to me and lifted her off my lap. Together we swung around and slammed into the wall I'd just been sitting against.

This time with me on top.

The metal cuff dug into my wrist hard enough to make the metal pipe it was attached to groan. I didn't care about the pain. All I cared about was ruining her.

I unclasped her pants, biting her lower lip as I slid her zipper down. She did the rest, and soon they were bunched down by her ankles. Elisha kicked her feet, carelessly inching them off one foot at a time.

My cupped hand was nearly scalded by the heat that came off her pussy. A low moan escaped her as I let my fingers rest heavily against her lower lips. Her wetness bled through the thin cotton panties.

It got me so fucking turned on.

I kissed her from collarbone to her jawline, then bit her ear. "I want you to know," I whispered into her ear, "I heard you in bed that night in the motel, after you left me locked up in the bathroom."

Her eyes widened. A delicious smile parted her full lips.

In response, Elisha stuck her hand down my pants, grabbed my cock, and squeezed. I moved the fabric of her panties aside and hovered over her lower lips. Nothing between us but air and time.

"Every stroke." I dragged a finger between her soaked lips. "Every moan. I heard it all." I pushed lightly at her clit, but with mounting pressure. She moaned through gritted teeth as if I'd commanded her to.

"I'd hoped you would," Elisha said through labored breaths. She impatiently freed my cock and started stroking it.

I traced the outline of her jaw to her chin, then used my bottom teeth to tilt her head back. "I know," I said, wrapping my teeth around her soft neck.

Hearing her gasp at the pressure sent waves of near-uncontrollable lust rippling inside me. I was on the verge of snapping my bonds, and if that happened, I wouldn't be able to control myself. I needed to feel all of her.

She worked my cock faster, squeezing even tighter. My teeth trembled around her throat. I thrust two fingers into her slick opening.

I released her throat to watch her reaction as I pushed deeper into her silky tunnel. I wanted to see her every twitch and furrow, to read the pleasure that rolled off her in waves. Her muscles tightened around my fingers, trying to crush them. I used it, sliding them in and out in a curling motion. I laid my thumb over her clit, motionless except for the constant pushing.

She tried rubbing the fat head of my cock against her pussy, but I stayed just out of reach. I loved watching her squirm for it. The closer she bucked, the more I pulled away.

Even now, she was too shy to ask for what she wanted.

"Do you want me to fuck you?"

She bit her lip and nodded. "Yes."

I didn't press her on it this time, but if the stars aligned and we ever did fuck again, I was going to make her beg for more. Thoughts of her screaming my name made my cock throb.

Sliding my fingers out, I wrapped my hands around hers and jerked myself off. Elisha tightly grabbed her tit and pinched her nipple "Please," she whimpered.

I was awed by her innocence and loved that she liked it a little rough.

I toyed with her, putting in just the tip before cruelly pulling it out. I dragged the head of my cock from the top of her clit to the bottom of her pussy, occasionally dipping in. Her face contorted with the torture. Seeing how badly she wanted it made my stomach muscles tight.

When I couldn't stand it any longer, I pushed in. She was soaked and beyond ready for me.

"Oh God, I can't...." Her hands dug into my shoulders with every inch I gave her. She moaned, pressing her eyes shut and burying her chin into her chest. I'd gone slowly, so as not to hurt her too much. When she thought she'd taken all of me, she sighed in relief.

Her hands slid my jeans down enough to squeeze my ass. I pushed into her until her eyes were on the verge of crossing.

"Yes." Her lips formed the word, but she couldn't spare the air for any noise to actually escape.

I flexed my cock in her tight walls as I lost myself, and all sense of time and place. There was only Elisha. Every glorious inch of her burned into my mind. It melted me. I put my arm behind her back and hoisted her toward me, changing the angle.

Fuck, she felt amazing. Whenever she brought me to the cusp, I slowed back down with long, deliberate thrusts. I listened to her body, watching and reading her, feeling the way her stomach and hips pulsed.

Minutes… hours… maybe even days sailed by, I had no idea. The only thing I knew was that we moved in rhythmic harmony, and I could fuck her forever.

I felt her get close. Her body trembled from a thousand fireworks set to charge off and explode. Sweat beaded and ran down my temples. I rode the wave, and when she climaxed, she took me with her. Her body tensed and coiled around my cock. I went to pull out, but she held me close, refusing to let me.

"No," she said with a wide breathless smile.

"Let's give Ella a sibling," I panted, all teeth with a low growl from still being in the throes of coming.

Two filthy, sweating bodies collapsed atop one another in primal joy. I rolled onto my back and lay next to her. For a while we just breathed, allowing reality to seep its way back into our lives.

"Wow" was all she could muster between great deep breaths. Elisha slid off her panties and tossed them.

I was completely content and didn't have anything to say. Between the stresses of raising a baby, starting a new bounty hunting company, and me joining the Steel Veins, we both needed some ugly, messy fucking. It felt fantastic to let go with the woman I loved and trusted like no other, it was akin to finally setting down a heavy backpack after a month-long hike.

I looked at Elisha. She smiled back and glowed with exhaustion and satiation.

When I thought the moment couldn't get more perfect, she rolled onto her side and hugged me. The side of her face was pressed against the steady, unburdened rise and fall of my chest. I immediately realized that I needed that as bad as the sex.

It hit me every once in a while that we were partners in all things. After feeling so alone for so many years, I now had someone I could truly rely on. Another kid, trials and tribulations of being an entrepreneur in an unsteady world... none of that mattered. I brushed the hair out of her eyes and looked deep into her beautiful eyes and saw only love and acceptance.

"As long as I have you, everything will be all right," I said, more to myself than to her. She smiled in return, not needing to speak the words in order to tell me how right I was.

"Better together," she cooed instead, squeezing me tighter.

"Always."

# About The Author

Jackson Kane is a professional stuntman, athlete, romance author, and above all else, a hopeless romantic. From American Ninja Warrior to some of your favorite films, Jackson brings a unique writing style forged from countless harrowing adventures.

He's a lover of travel, his fans, his romance author peers, dulce de leche, and all things beautifully weird and interesting. He invites you to relax, have a pisco sour, and let him thrill and excite you in a way no other author can. Jackson will show you what the world looks like through the eyes of a genuine Bad Boy.

Come with him, and…
DARE TO READ DANGEROUSLY

# Craving More?

BLOW OUT (STEEL VEINS 1)
BURN UP (STEEL VEINS 2)
RAW DEAL (STEEL VEINS 3)
MY HOLIDAY SECRET

# About the Publisher

Hot Tree Publishing opened its doors in 2015 with an aspiration to bring quality fiction to the world of readers. With the initial focus on romance and a wide spread of romance subgenres, Hot Tree Publishing has since opened their first imprint, Tangled Tree Publishing, specializing in crime, mystery, suspense, and thriller.

Firmly seated in the industry as a leading editing provider to independent authors and small publishing houses, Hot Tree Publishing is the sister company to Hot Tree Editing, founded in 2012. Having established in-house editing and promotions, plus having a well-respected market presence, Hot Tree Publishing endeavors to be a leader in bringing quality stories to the world of readers.

Interested in discovering more amazing reads brought to you by Hot Tree Publishing? Head over to the website for information:

WWW.HOTTREEPUBLISHING.COM